RESCUER

DOMS OF MOUNTAIN BEND

BOOK 4

BJ Wane

Editors:
Kate Richards & Nanette Sipes

Cover Design & Formatting:
Joe Dugdale (sylv.net)

PUBLISHED BY BLUE DAHLIA

DISCLAIMER

This contemporary romantic suspense contains adult themes such as power exchange and sexual scenes. Please do not read if these offend you.

DEDICATION

This book is dedicated to my awesome editors, Kate Richardson and Nanette Sipes, and my wonderful beta readers, Sandie Buckley, Gaynor Jones, and Kathy Heare Watts. Thank you so much, ladies – I couldn't do it without you!

CONTENTS

PROLOGUE

Eighteen-year-old Amie Buchanon pulled up the hood on her poncho, shielding her tear-ravaged face as much as she could from the light, dreary drizzle falling on the group of mourners gathered around the flower-draped coffin. Flanked by her parents, she stood to the side of the family seated under the tent. Amie grieved along with her best friend, Myla, over the suicidal death of Myla's brother, Mike. Although, according to Myla, he had some help going over the rail of the balcony of his twentieth-floor apartment.

And Myla vowed when she had the means, skills, and proof to confront then kill Cal Miller, she wouldn't hesitate. That scared Amie. She couldn't bear to lose Myla, too. The two of them were closer than sisters, Mike the older brother she never knew she wanted, their parents the best of friends. Amie couldn't imagine her life without Myla, even more so now that Mike was gone.

Amie's dad took her elbow, and she gave him a smile of gratitude, her heart turning over at his drawn face and red-rimmed eyes. Both her parents had considered Myla and Mike family ever since Amie and Myla had bonded and become inseparable at the age of two, when they'd moved in next door to the Nortons. As an only child, Amie loved Myla and Mike as both friends and the siblings she'd never had, even though there were times growing up Mike was more the irritating, too-protective, older brother, putting a crimp in their fun.

The mournful echo of bagpipes filled the air as the service ended, and she released a relieved sigh. She'd never met Mike's lover, Cal, but prayed Myla would come to her senses once her initial shock and grief became easier to live with. The police and coroner ruled his death a suicide, and their parents were also convinced their son had been despondent enough over the breakup of his first serious relationship with the older man to take such a drastic step.

They walked toward the Nortons as the family rose and thanked the minister. "Be right back," she told her dad.

"Take your time, hon." He nodded, squeezing her shoulder.

Amie smiled, grateful for their understanding, then turned to go to Myla who met her halfway between the plot and the waiting funeral cars. Throwing her arms around her, she felt her shudder. Pulling away, she asked, "How are you holding up, Myla?"

Her friend's gray eyes were as stormy as the overcast laden skies. "I'll be fine once he's as dead as my brother," she hissed.

Her heart breaking, Amie's eyes grew teary again. She was always the peacemaker between her and Myla, calmly settling their disputes with practical suggestions that Myla usually rolled her eyes at before reluctantly conceding to go along. If only she would react like that now and agree with her it was best to stifle such thoughts.

"You can't let anyone hear you talk like that, especially your parents. Haven't they gone through enough?" Okay, she wasn't above piling on the guilt when desperate.

"And that's the only reason I haven't gone after the bastard. I told you about the bruises he left on Mike and his lame excuses. How can you not want to seek justice for him?"

Hurt swirled in her gaze and tore at Amie's conscience. "If there was proof, or if the police were looking at his death differently, I'd help any way I could, but, Myla, you're the only person who thinks Mike's ex is guilty. You have to let that go. You just don't want to blame Mike, and neither do I, but facts are facts."

Squaring her shoulders, Myla's eyes turned cold. "I'll *never* let it go."

She walked away without looking back, and Amie wondered if she'd already lost her best friend.

Twelve years later

"I can't believe you're going to go through with this." Amie paced Myla's bedroom floor, wringing her hands, casting disbelieving glances toward the array of skimpy outfits strewn across her bed. "Are you really going to that place wearing one of those?" She couldn't imagine parading around in front of other people dressed in nothing but a butt-baring thong and push-up bra that didn't even fully cover the nipples.

"Yep." Myla picked up a teal satin teddy Amie had to admit was a tempting number to wear *under* something. "This would look great on you and would go well with your eyes. It's always good to emphasize your best feature."

Plopping onto the overstuffed chair in the corner, she glared at her friend. "Quit changing the subject, Myla." Her voice caught. "I'm scared for you."

She let out an unconcerned sigh. It was just like her to make light of Amie's concern. "I'll be fine. These private clubs are known for good security and strict rules. *He* wouldn't dare try anything there."

"But you would, is that what you're saying?"

"Yep, that's what I'm saying," she admitted without a trace of guilt for deceiving Amie all this time. That hurt more than her keeping her research into private clubs a secret from Amie after learning Cal Miller was a member of the two clubs in the Omaha area.

Myla hadn't given up on her quest to see Cal pay for Mike's death, one way or another. For a few years, as a favor to Myla, Amie had agreed to help her look for evidence of his guilt. All through college, they'd spoken to Mike's friends, neighbors in his apartment building, and his co-workers. They'd gone through his things, leaving nothing untouched before the Nortons gave everything away. Amie was majoring in medical billing technology and Myla in website design and graphics, and they used their increasing computer skills to research Miller.

All to no avail in finding anything that connected him to Mike's death.

They'd graduated without anything to go on and that's when Amie had said enough. She was out. Myla had agreed, which made her suspicious, but it wasn't until these last few months she learned her sneaky friend had researched the BDSM lifestyle, intending to corner Cal at the local clubs.

Amie gave Myla a sardonic look. "What exactly are you going to do if you see Cal there? Accuse him of helping your brother commit suicide?"

Shrugging, Myla stepped into the miniscule thong Amie wouldn't be caught dead in, not with the extra weight she carried. "That, and let him know I'm not going anywhere or giving up until he pays," she said.

"That'll scare him," she returned dryly until Myla pulled a small pistol out of her bedside drawer, sending her worry for her friend through the roof. "You wouldn't, would you?"

"In a heartbeat. Don't fret. I've been taking lessons at the firing range. Cute instructor, another reason to keep going back," she teased.

Amie wasn't in the mood to smile. "You're willing to commit murder and spend the rest of your life in prison?" She stood on shaky legs, her entire body vibrating with disbelief.

"Oh, I'm sure I can goad him into going for me first. Then I can claim self- defense." Her smug look said she'd thought of everything.

"You think you have an answer for everything, but since when do things always go according to plan? I want no part of this. Don't tell me anything else." She pivoted to leave but paused at the doorway to turn her head for one last parting shot, one last attempt to get through to her. "If you do this, it'll destroy your parents."

Her face went white. "That was low, Amie," she snapped.

"That was the truth, and you know it." Her shoulders slumped, and she sighed, giving up. Their bond went too deep for her to leave on such a sour note. "Call me, no matter how late. With luck, you'll meet a hot Dom who will change your focus."

She snorted, smirking. "I'm as much a geek as you and doubt anyone will notice me. Later."

Amie drove back to her apartment wondering how Myla planned to confront Cal Miller if she found him at that club. It wasn't like she could goad him into going for her there in front of a room full of naked people. The image that popped into her head almost made her smile. With luck, she'd realize the stupidity of her idea once she got there, or, better yet, Miller wouldn't show up, thwarting her plans altogether.

Even though the odds of Myla succeeding in her ridiculous, risky quest tonight were low, Amie couldn't relax once she got home. Keeping her phone close, she stuck to her regular Friday night routine of popcorn and a movie. Her two obsessions were old thrillers and butterflies, as her extensive movie collection, six butterfly tattoos, and thirty-one cut-glass figurines could prove. More often than not, Myla joined her for a movie, and she'd been the one to talk her into getting her first tattoo. The finished ink of the rainbow butterfly on her ankle had hooked her on adding the skin art to her collection of the colorful winged species.

Settling on the sofa with a bowl of buttered popcorn, she used the remote to turn on *House of Wax*, a Vincent Price favorite of hers, wishing Myla were with her. She stuffed her face, trying not to fret, but that didn't stop her from nearly jumping out of her skin two hours later when her phone pealed at the same moment Vincent got in one last scare.

"*Crap.*" Muting the television, she grabbed her cell, a sense of foreboding tightening her muscles when she saw Myla's parents' home phone on the caller ID. "Hello."

Steve Norton's broken voice describing Myla's near-fatal injuries in a car accident turned Amie's blood to ice. After assuring him she was on her way, she hung up and dashed out the door, her throat clogged with a ball of nausea. *Why didn't I try harder to stop her*? That was the only thought running through her head as she drove to Omaha's trauma center, praying Myla wasn't as bad as her father described.

Her first glimpse of her best friend through the glass partition in ICU told her those pleas had gone unanswered. The Norton's tearful hugs and despairing faces hinted her prognosis was as dire as they'd said. Tears rolled down Amie's cheeks as she gazed at Myla's battered face and bandage-wrapped head.

Head injury. Internal bleeding. Broken leg. The list seemed endless, leaving her to wonder if there was any hope. *Why, Myla? Why wouldn't you listen to me and let it go?*

"What did the doctors say?" she asked as they moved to wait in a private waiting room.

Myla's mother, Laura, shook her head. "They won't come out and say anything definitive yet. All we've gotten is they don't know, or they're waiting on more tests, or time will tell. Oh God, I just can't lose another child." She turned to sob in her husband's arms, her devastation breaking Amie's heart.

If she weren't so worried about Myla, she would be furious with her for putting them all through this. With no other option, she called her parents, who promised to come right up, then settled in for a long vigil of wait and see.

One month later

Amie looked down the gun's barrel, squinted, and pulled the trigger. The bullet hit the cardboard cutout of a person in the arm, her best shot yet. She sent Matt a beaming smile, pulling off the protective head set covering her ears.

"Admit it. I'm good enough to hold my own."

His brown eyes clouded with worry. "You have developed a steady hand and managed to hit your targets *under these calm conditions.*" He further emphasized his point by circling his arm around the secure, well-monitored firing range. "Our targets aren't attacking you, threatening you, or even talking. If you insist on going through with your plan, you'll end up like Myla, or worse."

Her shoulders slumped, and she handed him

the pistol, handle first. "I have to try. You of all people should understand."

Matt White cared almost as much for Myla as Amie and was as devastated over her condition and struggles as she and the Nortons were. Defying the odds, Myla had survived, and, last week, had recovered enough to get moved into a rehabilitation facility. She would need extensive therapy, and her negative attitude wouldn't make it any easier. Neither Matt nor Amie would give up on her, though, especially not after the police investigation turned up evidence she was run off the road by another car, a fact Myla confirmed.

That changed everything for Amie, and made her more susceptible when Myla had pleaded with her for justice five days ago when she'd visited her in the rehab for the first time.

Amie knocked then entered Myla's room, the bright sunshine pouring in from the large window overlooking the sprawling green lawn of the rehab facility as welcome as seeing her friend dressed and sitting in a chair. After over three weeks in the hospital, two surgeries, and numerous tests, she looked pale, thin, and bruised, but still much better than those first days.

"This place is much cheerier than the hospital.

How are you doing, Myla?" she asked, crossing the room to take the chair next to her.

"He did...this...to me," Myla stuttered, her struggle to talk just one of the things the rehab would address while she was here. With a shaky hand, she reached over and gripped Amie's arm, her eyes fierce with an avenging need Amie now felt more deeply than before, when it had been just Mike hurt by this man. "Please, Amie. You're...you... are all...I've got...my only...h...hope."

It broke her heart listening to her difficult speech, seeing the tears coursing down her sunken cheeks and the desperation etched on her face. She would do anything to help Myla now, or almost anything.

"I don't know what I can do, but I'll try. Maybe I can track his whereabouts and befriend him then get him to slip and admit something, but I won't agree to anything with the intention of killing the man, Myla. I promise, I'll do what I have to for him to say something incriminating."

Her gaze turned sad, remorseful, and again tore at Amie's heart and conscience. "He's dan... gerous. First Mike,...now me." She shook her head, her eyes clouding. "Never...mind, Amie. Th...anks, but it's too...risky."

She didn't think her anger toward Cal Miller could get any stronger, but hearing the defeat in Myla's voice, seeing her put her concern for Amie ahead of her twelve-year quest to get justice for her brother, hardened Amie's resolve to do what she could for both of them. Now the tables were reversed, and it was her turn to convince Myla to support her.

"I'll be careful, and I've been taking firing lessons in case I need to protect myself. You know I'm not a risk taker." She didn't tell her she planned to push herself in that regard. Between turning thirty and the deliberate attempt on Myla's life, she was ready for some changes in her life. "Besides," she teased, "I'll get bored hanging around waiting for you to get out of here."

Myla's jaw went rigid, and her lips tightened, her stubborn look that Amie knew well. "You...you don't have the...hate...the anger...to succeed...and... I'm s....sorry. I realize I...can't ask...this of you.... not right...not safe."

"And now you know how I felt. Okay, if you promise to try hard to cooperate here, then I'll wait. Deal?"

Myla had promised but never followed through, growing more depressed and resentful with each day. Upset and frustrated, Amie now realized the full depth of what had driven her for twelve years to seek justice for her brother. She hadn't a clue what she could do, but desperation nonetheless shored up her resolve to see that this man paid for the sinful crimes that had hurt the ones she loved most.

It was her turn to seek justice for her friend.

Matt's voice dragged her attention back to him. "I do understand you wanting answers and to see him pay if you're sure he's the one. But it's wiser and safer to let the police handle it. Look where Myla's obsession with this guy has landed her, and how many have suffered because of it." He shook his head, his face reflecting sadness. "I wanted to marry her, still do. But she won't even discuss it now. She thinks she'll be a burden to me, but all I've ever wanted was to take care of her."

His tone conveyed a wealth of love, devotion, and so much pain, Amie hurt for him. Myla's stubbornness had contributed to her current ordeal, and accounted for Matt's broken heart, but she understood better than him what had driven her friend. Amie still missed Mike and mourned his death, so she could imagine the depth of Myla's loss. A cool breeze kicked up, reminding her fall was fast approaching, and her time frame to find and befriend Cal Miller where she'd tracked him down in Idaho was dwindling.

She'd never met the man and only had an old photo and his name to go on, but it'd been enough when combined with her computer skills to learn a lot about him and his habits. A man in his late forties of substantial financial means, the only thing she could discover that would interrupt his favorite sport of big game hunting was an occasional visit to the closest private club in the area. He rarely joined hunting groups, his accommodations were always for a single occupancy, yet his numerous guest memberships around the country indicated he enjoyed the company of others.

Or so she assumed since sex was an easy entertainment for such a man. Then again, what did she understand about the alternative practices except what she'd learned through research and reading? She could never stomach allowing him to touch her, but, given his relationship with Mike, that necessity wouldn't come into play anyway. Knowing Cal's preference for young men gave her the extra courage to take a stab at getting justice for Myla and Mike. The most she could hope for was to engage him in conversations that might lead to a slip of the tongue since he didn't know her.

A flimsy plan at best, but all Amie had to do was remember Mike's death and Myla's near-fatal accident to convince herself it was worth a try.

"Don't give up on her, Matt. Her recovery thus far has defied all the odds, and I don't doubt once she heals enough to gain her independence back, she'll come around. She loves you, too." Amie pivoted to pick up her purse from a bench behind them, the loud report of gunshots continuing to echo in the air. Saturdays were busy on the firing range. "I have to go, but I promise, I won't run off half- cocked. My plan is to get him to slip up, say anything incriminating I can give to the police. That will require me getting to know him, which, frankly, makes my skin crawl. These lessons were to ensure my ability to defend myself if he gets violent or physical. But I can't walk away this time. I'm sorry, I just can't."

"I know. That's what makes this all that much harder. I should be the one avenging her, but no matter how I look at it, it's foolish. Come on, I'll walk you out."

Foolish or not, a week later, Amie loaded up her car and started the two-day drive to the small town of Mountain Bend, the nearest place to where she'd tracked Miller's travel arrangements and hunting license for the next several weeks, and the closest to the private club, Spurs, where she hoped to come across him. She just prayed this didn't end up one of those rash decisions that bit her on the butt. For the most part, she'd outgrown her childhood penchant for landing herself into trouble she would invariably need rescuing from by acting without thinking first, but then, she'd never done anything this daring either.

Chapter One

"*Fuck.*"

Wildlife expert and parks ranger Ben Wilkins reached behind him for his rifle before sliding out of his state commissioned SUV. Dread churned in his gut as he approached the fallen elk with caution and slow-building fury. Down or not, the animal's size and weight could still pose a threat. The small clearing where the bull had managed to limp before his injured leg and blood loss forced him to collapse wasn't far off the open range where Ben had been patrolling. The animal's mournful braying, so different from the species' regular sounds, had alerted him to his distress.

Stopping a foot away, he eyed the bullet wounds in the right hind ankle and knee and the massive blood puddle on the ground. "The bastard is back." If this deliberate maiming and torture was the work of the same hunter Ben had tracked for weeks last spring, he vowed nothing would stop him from finding and arresting him this time.

Raising his rifle, he took aim and fired, ending the bull's misery, his heart heavy for both what the animal had endured and for being forced to put him down. Hunting for sport, meat, and hides was one thing, and something he participated in on occasion. But what this person did was nothing short of pure, evil cruelty. Turning from the carcass, he strode back to his vehicle, called for help in removing the elk, and settled back to wait. It wouldn't take long for a few other rangers nearby to get here, but Ben was damn glad it was Friday, and that he was off for the weekend. That would give him time to get himself under control and research whoever had fall hunting licenses.

It took four of them to haul the dead elk into the back of a truck, each of his co-workers as upset over the hunter's cruelty as Ben. They agreed to donate the meat to Boise's shelters before Carl and Dave took off to drop the elk at the butcher, leaving him with Neil Pollono, a new acquaintance and fellow ranger.

"Hell of a way to end the day," Neil said, eyeing the elk's dangling head off the end of the truck bed.

Ben checked the time then said, "Isn't it though?

I'm meeting Shawn to let him know about this guy. Will you be at Spurs later?" He was also a member of the private club outside of Mountain Bend that Neil had recently joined.

"I'm looking forward to it. Maybe Kathie will amuse me enough to get rid of the sour taste this has left."

Ben's lips curled. "Be careful. With Shawn, Dakota, and Clayton settling into committed relationships these past few months, you might be next. But Kathie isn't one of the subs wanting to go that route." Neil had found Spur's little troublemaker to his liking. He even enjoyed her temper tantrums and antics.

"I'm not either, so we'll make a good pair for now. Thanks. I'll see you there."

"I'll be about another two hours. Thanks for your help."

Ben slid behind the wheel of his vehicle and followed Neil down off the mountain slope and out onto the open range then turned his mind to more pleasant thoughts. He'd acquired a pair of malnourished miniature horses that needed attention this evening, bringing his total of adopted, neglected animals to twelve. With just twenty acres, he could only adopt a handful more without looking into buying additional land. The amount of grazing available for the now six horses, one longhorn steer, and two llamas was good, but he never could turn down a request for help from the SPCA or Humane Society when they called needing a foster or permanent home for a ranch animal. Each time he'd gone to answer a call, he'd been unable to resist bringing home a dog also, the staff ribbing him for being such a sucker for a pitiful face.

Maybe he was, he thought, pulling into the parking lot at the ranger's station. But other than socializing at Spurs on weekends, he preferred spending as much of his time outdoors and with animals. Since he'd turned thirty-six four months ago, his parents kept badgering him about settling down and giving them grandkids, but, so far, he hadn't met a woman who intrigued him enough to keep her close for long.

Ben filled out his report on a possible hunter intent on maiming then clocked out and drove to his place ten miles outside of Mountain Bend's city limits. His rustic ranch home was on the small size but just right for him. He'd bought it and the surrounding acreage from his parents when they moved to their lake home in Alabama to get away from the long Idaho winters. There were times when the snow was six feet deep with a wind chill of twenty below, and he sometimes wondered why the heck he stayed here. But all it took was a friendly wave from a stranger as he drove into town or the sight of the mountains across the grassland range dotted with a herd of shaggy-coated lumbering bison to remind him why he preferred this area and state over others.

Entering the house, he hung up his Stetson, greeting the dogs as they gathered around him with tails wagging. Next to family, they were the best thing to come home to after a long, difficult day. With his parents in Alabama, his closest relative was his sister, Clare, who lived in Boise.

"Come on, guys, let's get your treats."

He avoided glancing toward his brother's picture on the fireplace mantel as he crossed the hardwood floors into the kitchen. With the fifteen-year anniversary of Bart's death tomorrow, he didn't need any more reminders of his loss or the grief of losing his twin. Even after all this time, guilt still cramped his gut whenever he let himself think about the one time he wasn't there to rescue Bart from one of his wild stunts.

Growing up, the two of them had gotten into their share of scrapes and trouble, but it was always Bart who had gone beyond reckless fun and taken dangerous risks. They were just shy of turning eight when his brother had decided to taunt a bull moose, something they were taught never to do. Ben had saved him from getting trampled by leaping onto one of the horses in the same pasture and diverting the angry bull at the last moment.

On their tenth birthday, they'd gone ice fishing at their pond, but Bart hadn't been content to sit at the edge. Ignoring his warnings and pleas, he'd ventured onto the frozen top and had fallen through. Ben managed to pull him out by lying on his stomach. Bart had still developed pneumonia but at least hadn't drowned.

One night, a few years later, he'd tried talking his headstrong brother out of sneaking out to join in a midnight drag race, but Bart again refused to listen, forcing Ben to follow him. He'd arrived in time to watch his foolish twin take off at high speed down the county dirt road in his old pickup and to hear two of the older boys plotting to sabotage Bart's vehicle when he won against their friend. Satisfied with his victory, Bart agreed it was time to go after listening to what Ben had overheard.

To his dying day, Ben would regret leaving the ranch, and his brother, to attend the University of Idaho located three hundred miles north in

Moscow. Determined to earn degrees in both wildlife management and forestry, he'd chosen the best school for his career choices despite his misgivings about being that far away from his reckless twin. When Bart took off that summer to make his name on the rodeo circuit, Ben and their parents had begged him to be careful and wished him luck. Two years later, after staying up late partying and drinking, he'd taken on the challenge of being the first to best a mean-tempered bull and paid for his cocky bravado undermined by his poor, morning-after concentration with his life.

Shoving aside his melancholy, Ben gave the dogs a rawhide each then filled their food and water bowls. With his friend Shawn's help, he had installed a dog door that gave his dogs freedom to go out in a secure, enclosed area while he was gone. He'd taken in Sheba, a German shepherd, the same time Shawn adopted his two shepherds from a rescue, all three looking much better after a few months of a steady, healthy diet. Tending to the elk had cut into his time, so he only had ten minutes to throw a ball a few times before he checked on the other animals then drove into town.

Fewer than seven thousand called the small, renovated mining town of Mountain Bend home year-round, but, during the warmer months and hunting seasons, the campgrounds, cabins, and B&B filled up fast. Passing the sheriff's office, he noticed Shawn's cruiser gone from his parking spot out front and continued on toward the Watering Hole. Loud music drowned out the low hum of voices and the clack of pool table activity as he entered the bar and wound his way through the crowded tables to the corner one Shawn occupied.

"The Friday night crowd is out early," Ben stated. Taking a seat, he crossed one ankle over his opposite thigh and hooked his Stetson on his bent knee.

"So are we. What's up?" Shawn asked, signaling the waitress.

Ben told him about the elk and his suspicions it might be the work of the same hunter they never found last spring. "I'd hate to think there were two such sick fucks like that out there, but it's a possibility."

"Unfortunately, there's no shortage of sick fucks," Shawn replied, his gray eyes turning dark.

"At least you don't have to worry about the one who came after Lisa." Ben suspected he was thinking about the ordeal his fiancé, Lisa's half-brother had put her through. Brian Pomeroy had ended up paying the ultimate price for his crimes of stalking and attempted murder.

Shawn nodded. “One down, but there’s always another to take his place. I can send out a notice about this perv, have everyone keep their ears open to any rumors, but you guys are in a better position to find him. Get Dakota to track with you again.”

Dakota Smith was the best tracker in the area, as well as one of the owners of Spurs and the Rolling Hills Ranch, along with Shawn and their friend, Clayton Trebek. A native of the area, Ben was a year ahead of them in school when the local rancher, Buck Cooper, had taken in the three foster boys at the age of fifteen. But it wasn’t until they’d all joined Spurs that he’d gotten to really know them.

The waitress, a young college-age girl named Angela, arrived to take their orders, her eyes lingering on Ben before she smiled and promised to be right back with their drinks.

“They’re getting younger and more brazen,” Ben muttered, not flattered by the girl’s blatant look of interest.

“What, you don’t go for the ones young enough to be your daughter?” Shawn mocked with a teasing glint in his eyes.

“Hey, I’m not...okay, maybe I am old enough

to have fathered someone her age. Shit, that doesn't even bear thinking about. And no, you know damn good and well I don't go for them that young any more than you," he retorted.

"But I've settled down with a nice girl."

A kernel of envy knotted in Ben's gut, but he shoved it aside. He was happy for his friend and figured the upcoming anniversary of Bart's death was responsible for his moodiness lately.

"I heard you've sealed your commitment. Congratulations, Lisa is a nice girl. Too bad she doesn't have a sister," he returned, imagining a sibling with the same striking white-blonde hair and bright-green eyes as the sheriff's schoolteacher, Lisa.

Shawn scooped up some peanuts from the bowl on the table, his lips curling in a grin. "Poppy does, though, and last I heard, she's coming for a visit soon."

"And have Dakota breathing down my neck. I don't think so. To hear him talk, he's almost as protective of Rebecca as he is of Poppy," he returned dryly. "Besides, isn't she around twenty?"

"Twenty-four, so your only hurdle would be Dakota."

"He's a damn big hurdle, in size and

temperament."

The waitress returned and set down their beers.

"Thank you," Ben told her, trying to stay polite without encouraging the girl.

"You're welcome. If you need anything else, let me know." She punctuated that remark by setting a cocktail napkin with her phone number written in a fancy scroll down in front of Ben.

With a sigh, Ben picked it up and handed it back to her. "Do us both a favor and give this to that young man at the bar. He's been eyeing your every move."

She frowned and swiveled to look at the guy who was much closer to her age. "Huh, I didn't even see him since I don't work the bar."

She walked away without another word, and Ben released a relieved breath. "Thank God we don't have another Sharon Mize on our hands."

The previous waitress had pursued their friend Clayton long after he'd stopped taking her out and then had turned her jealous anger on Skye, Clayton's new girl. None of them knew what Clayton had said to her to get her to back off, but she'd taken a job in Boise shortly after and no one missed her.

Shawn took a drink then shook his head with a rueful look. "I sure as hell don't miss those complications from being single. Then again, I've usually stuck to socializing at the club. Speaking of which, we need to get out there soon for our meeting."

As much as he enjoyed the company and the cold brew sliding down, Ben found the temptation to excuse himself from attending tonight hard to resist. His mood had dipped since leaving work, the suffering the elk had gone through weighing on him. His current disposition wasn't conducive to socializing, let alone staying attentive to a sub's needs. But going home and spending the evening brooding over things he couldn't change didn't sound appealing either.

Shawn cocked his head, the meager light above the table enough to bring out the red tint in his dark-mahogany hair. "Something wrong?"

As both a Dom and the sheriff, Shawn never missed much, a trait Ben didn't admire at that moment. "No, just coming down off a long week." He took the last swig of his beer and set the bottle down before pushing away from the table. "I'll see you out there."

Spurs was located in a small clearing surrounded by woods a half mile off the main highway between Boise and Mountain Bend, the gravel parking lot already full when Ben arrived. The previous owner, Randy Daniels, had sold the club to Shawn, Dakota, and Clayton when he'd filed for divorce from his unfaithful wife and had wanted to get away after that blow. Another reason to remain single, he thought, sliding out of his vehicle. Women were fickle creatures, delightful most of the time, but, when they turned on you, look out.

Striding up to the front doors, he gave himself a mental kick for the thought that lumped all women in the same category as Randy's ex. He blamed his melancholy mood and entered through the double doors, opting to leave his hat on as he continued across the wide foyer and opened the door into the main room. The three owners, along with Simon and new member, Neil, sat around a large table in the middle of the seating area, a few other Doms seated at the table next to them. The cavernous room was quiet except for the low murmurs of their deep voices, but an hour from now it would resonate with music, low moans, and high-pitched wails of BDSM play, activity he enjoyed listening to, participating in, and watching.

Ben noted he was the last to arrive as he strode across the hardwood floor. He hadn't thought he'd dallied on his way out here, but maybe he had without realizing he was taking his time. Another sign he should have stayed home tonight. Grabbing a chair from a vacant table, he turned it and straddled the seat, resting his arms across the top, keeping quiet so he didn't interrupt Clayton.

"Hey, Ben. We've just started, and I have the schedule for monitoring and bartending here." Clayton passed the papers to Dakota. "The timetable goes to the end of the year, but anyone who needs to change a date, get someone to switch with you or let us know. The other thing on the agenda is a fall fundraiser Cody McCullough and his wife, Olivia, have asked us to host. For those who are new in the last six-to-eight months, the two oldest McCullough brothers were regulars here before they relocated to their family ranch in Snake Valley. They visit a couple of times a year when they're in the area for supplies or auctions."

"Are they wanting the proceeds to go to the women's shelter again?" Ben asked, remembering the other time they'd raised money for Olivia's cause.

Shawn nodded. "Yep, and we want to make it an annual event, but that needs to be approved by the majority, keeping in mind the local ranches' obligations to take their turn hosting one of the summer picnics and a Big Brothers Big Sisters fundraiser. Most of us here have spreads and sign up for one of the town picnics every summer. We also take turns hosting the annual charity event, which, granted, isn't often given the number of ranches on the list."

Several members spoke up, offering their support for the project, and Clayton called for a show of hands. After everyone agreed, Neil asked, "What did the McCulloughs have in mind?"

"They left it up to us. Sub auctions are popular, or a game night where you have to pay to play each one," Shawn suggested.

Ben's interest perked up at that idea. "That could be fun. We're good at getting creative, and, if we plan together, pool our ideas, we could come up with quite the variety."

Simon's mouth tilted on one side. "I'm liking this more and more."

Dakota shifted his black eyes toward Simon. "Nothing too sadistic, Risch." When the six-foot-four, quietest member spoke, everyone listened.

Despite Dakota's stern voice, Simon grinned. "I'm a pussycat."

Everyone chuckled at that since Simon was the strictest Dom and insisted any sub who scened with him adhere by all the rules, no exceptions. When

Dakota didn't lighten up, Simon dropped his smile, his gaze hardening. "C'mon, Smith. You know I'm careful and always respect their limits. You've just gotten mellow since you turned so protective over Poppy."

Dakota blew out a breath and grumbled, "You're right. Sorry."

Ben had never thought he'd see the gruff Native American settle down with one woman, let alone demonstrate such worry and care over her. He almost felt sorry for Poppy, given the way Dakota hovered, but her feisty nature and stubborn streak ensured he didn't trample on her independence.

"It sounds like everyone is favoring a game night," Clayton said. "Anyone who wants on the planning committee, let me know. Last order of business is a reminder of guest night next weekend. So far, we only have one signup, but that could change."

Drew Zimmerman stood and stretched, saying, "If too many more Masters follow you, Dakota, and Shawn into a committed relationship, there won't be enough left to bother with holding guest nights."

Ben flashed him a grin. "You could ask Jen to let you fill in."

"Yeah, right," someone muttered with a

chuckle.

Drew returned Ben's teasing grin. "Since I'm as possessive of my wife as she is of me, I'll leave the newbies to you."

"Speaking of which..." Shawn scraped his chair back as several women entered. "Ben, you're up next as guide to our guest. Meeting adjourned."

Watching Shawn, Dakota, and Clayton greeting their girls, Ben experienced a familiar tug of loss. The connection that came with having someone in his life who knew him inside and out, someone he could talk to, turn to in need was what he missed most since Bart's death. He hadn't found that special affinity with anyone else; neither between him and any of his friends, nor with a woman. Not to say he didn't have close male and female friends, and he'd certainly enjoyed the company of numerous women, along with their bodies, and, with some, their submission.

But no one had come close to snagging his interest then ensnaring his emotions the way he and his brother had been bonded. His twin would have understood Ben's anger on behalf of the elk's suffering, his need to vent, lash out at the deliberate cruelty. They were both on the wrestling team in high school, and Ben had made the cut in college.

Grappling with someone before showing up tonight would have gone a long way to ease his tense muscles from his still simmering fury.

Ben rose as Drew walked over. "That's no way to start the evening or the weekend. Shawn mentioned you came across an injured elk today."

"Not the best way to end the week, but I'll get the bastard."

"No doubt. Everyone around here is all for the sport of hunting as it keeps the numbers down, and a conscientious hunter will harvest the meat. Not this guy, huh?"

They started across the room toward the bar as Ben replied, "No, not this guy. On a happier note, I don't believe I've congratulated Lisa yet."

Drew chuckled. "I recognize that smirk. Go for it while I escort Jen over to the new bondage chair. She mentioned how scary it looked."

Ben lifted a brow, his lips curling at the corners. "Now I can say I recognize that leer. I'll try to come by and see how she fares. I haven't seen the new bondage bed upstairs yet. Have you?"

Shrugging, Drew scanned the open doors to the upstairs private rooms. "I haven't gotten the chance. That room was booked solid last weekend and is again tonight. It has been ever since word went out about the new acquisitions in the monthly newsletter."

An hour from now, those doors would be closed, the rooms occupied by members who enjoyed watching but preferred privacy for their play. The addition of the second level had paid for itself with the influx of new members over the past months.

"There's Jen now," Drew said when they reached the bar the same time his wife entered the club. He waved her over.

Settling on a stool next to Lisa, Shawn's girl, Ben lifted a finger to get the sheriff's attention before focusing on his fiancée. "I hear congratulations are in order for you two," he stated.

Shawn approached and handed him his beer. He nudged his hat back with one thumb and eyed him, wearing a curious frown. "You already passed that on earlier."

"Not to Lisa." Cocking his head, he waited for Shawn's permission, which he gave in the form of a short nod and glint in the gaze he turned on Lisa.

Her slim brows, two shades darker than her light blonde hair, dipped in a perplexed look. Then her green eyes widened as he leaned over, cupped her nape, and drew her toward him to meet his descending mouth. Out of respect, he kept it short, a slow brush of his lips over hers and an even slower taste of her plump, lower lip with his tongue before releasing her.

Lisa turned her head toward Shawn, getting ready to question him when Ben brought her face back around using his knuckles under her chin. "Congratulations, Lisa. Master Shawn is a lucky man."

"Oh, well, thank you." She narrowed her eyes at Shawn. "You could have said something."

"Where would the fun be in that?" he drawled.

A sly look crossed her face before she slid off the stool. "You're right. It was much more fun experiencing what a good kisser Master Ben is by getting taken by surprise. Thank you, Master Ben."

Shawn watched her stroll to a table and join Kathie and Poppy. "I have to remember she doesn't like surprises."

Ben smiled. From what he'd observed, Lisa was a delightful sexual submissive yet no one's doormat. The same could be said for the other two owners of Spurs about the women they'd recently committed to. It was as much fun to watch Poppy stand up to Dakota as it was to see her turn to putty when he bound and tormented her slender body. Clayton and Skye were still exploring their new relationship, but now that her memory had returned, she wasn't as tense around him or others.

Leaning a hip against the bar, Shawn eyed Ben with curiosity. "You've been quiet tonight. Anything on your mind other than the possibility of a sadistic hunter nearby?"

"Don't you have enough to deal with without probing for more?" Ben didn't mind him asking since he was as close to a good friend as he could claim since Bart's death, but that didn't mean he wanted to answer.

Shawn shrugged. "I've always got time for a friend, and I know this is a tough time of year for you."

"I appreciate that," Ben replied, blowing out a breath.

Mountain Bend hadn't grown much in population in the last fifteen years, so almost everyone over the age of thirty remembered Bart's tragic death at the young age of twenty-one. He could still recall the difficulty of going anywhere those first few months without getting stopped by well-meaning people offering condolences. The sharp twists of gut-wrenching pain he experienced for months afterward whenever he heard his brother's name mentioned had lessened over the years but not the acute sense of loss.

Determined to blow off his moodiness, he rose with a nod at Shawn. “Let me spell you early since I don’t have anyone waiting for me.”

“If you’re sure, I’ll take you up on that.” Shawn came around the end of the bar that ran along the south wall and clapped him on the shoulder as they traded places. “Let me know if you need anything.”

“Will do.”

What Ben needed, Shawn couldn’t provide, but he was grateful for the well-meaning show of support.

Chapter Two

Amie's headlights picked up the Welcome to Mountain Bend sign late Saturday night, and she breathed a sigh of relief. She'd found driving alone down two-lane country roads after dark spooky, the small amount of traffic and vast openness unsettling, and the quietness eerie. There were a lot of rural towns in Nebraska, but she'd grown up in Omaha, a city of just under half a million, and was more used to city life. Boise wasn't far, and she could have booked a place to stay there, but when she'd come across the tourist attractions in and around the area and the refurbished, Miner's Junction Bed and Breakfast had popped up, she couldn't resist staying in the quaint, century-old inn.

As she drove past a newer housing area, she checked the GPS for directions to the bed-and-breakfast where she had planned for a month's stay, wondering what she'd find to do in a town so small when she wasn't working or searching for Cal. The private club, Spurs, was only open on Friday and Saturday nights, and she hoped to come across Cal there. If not, she would have to come up with a plan B, and it was always when she tried to improvise or fly by the seat of her pants without Myla that she landed in trouble. Since her best friend had always been around, or close enough to rush to her aid, Amie had never gotten herself into too much of a pickle, but taking off on her own to help the friend who had always been there for her was a first. She would need to tread carefully if she wanted to get back home unscathed.

Winding her way through an older residential section, she found the charming wood-planked, renovated nineteenth-century home with no problem and pulled to a stop out front. The well-lit cobbled path leading up to the door cut through the darkness of her late arrival. Hoping the proprietor meant it when she assured Amie someone would be there to check her in around this time, she grabbed her purse and overnight bag, locked her car, and went inside.

Just like on the website pictures, the foyer and wide staircase off to the side boasted the original dark-walnut woodwork, the vintage brass six-light chandelier above her shedding enough illumination to guide her toward the podium near a narrow hall. Tapping the bell, she waited for the footsteps coming down the hall to reveal a middle-aged woman wearing a white apron over a T-shirt and jeans, her rosy face smudged with a streak of flour.

"Sorry, I didn't hear the front door. You must be Amie Buchanon. I'm Grace Whitticker." Grace blew a breath upward to slide some loose hairs out of her eyes, and, when that failed, she ran the back of her hand across her forehead, leaving another white smear.

"I am. I'm sorry for my late arrival. Ms. Zimmerman said it would be okay..."

"Oh heavens, yes. She and Drew are out for the evening, but me and my girls are always here until at least midnight preparing for the Sunday brunch that always draws a crowd." Grace turned an open ledger around and handed her a pen. "Just sign in, and I'll take you upstairs. The other three rooms are booked, so you'll have some company come morning."

Amie appreciated the woman's friendliness after her long, tiring trip. "I thought something smelled wonderful and assumed it was an apple-cinnamon candle or potpourri. Was I wrong?"

"Afraid so. I just pulled a tray of apple cinnamon

scones from the oven. You be sure to come down and go through the buffet in the morning. All breakfasts are included with your room, and that goes for the much bigger selection on Sunday. Here's your key." She handed over an old-fashioned, bronze skeleton key, and Amie loved the continued authenticity of the furnishings. "Do you have more luggage? I can send the girls out to get it."

"Please, don't bother. I have all I need for tonight in this bag, and I'm too tired to unpack tonight. Thanks for the offer." Picking up her suitcase, she followed Grace toward the stairs.

"It's quiet here at night," Grace said over her shoulder as she started up the staircase. "You won't have a problem sleeping. You're the first room on the right, and each one has its own bath. The owners, Drew and Jen, live next door, but if you need anything in the next hour or so, come on down and follow the hall to the kitchen. If not, welcome to Mountain Bend and good night, dear."

"Thanks, Grace."

Amie let herself into the small room dominated by a four-poster double bed covered with an old-fashioned, handmade quilt in shades of antique-white, navy, and cranberry that complemented the wine-colored drapes at the narrow French doors and the matching carpet. Two bedside lamps cast an amber glow around the room. She placed her suitcase on the hope chest at the foot of the bed, extracted her toiletries, and padded into the bathroom to wash her face and brush her teeth. Ten minutes later, she slid into the bed with a sigh, turned off the lamps, and drifted to sleep hoping this trip and disruption in her life proved worth the effort and risks for Myla.

There was nothing she wanted more than to return to Omaha with something concrete to take down Cal Miller for the pain and heartache he'd caused everyone she loved.

****

A stream of early morning sunlight penetrated the white curtains hanging between the French door drapes, brightening the room before Amie was fully awake. Blinking against the glare, she glanced at the bedside travel clock, her eyes going wide at seeing it was already after nine. She never slept this late. As she rolled out of the comfortable bed, she wondered if exhaustion was to blame or the culmination of weeks of stress coming to a head. Whatever the reason, she stretched and went into the bathroom feeling pretty darn good.

Amie stripped off her nightshirt and panties

and took a quick shower, her stomach rumbling the whole time, reminding her how long it had been since she'd eaten. After blow drying her hair and scooping the thick, shoulder-length waves back into a wide clip, she slipped on her jeans and retrieved a knit pullover top from her overnight case. Since the sun was out, she hoped the temperature was doable for sightseeing around town on foot. She figured the more she got out and about, the better her chances of coming across Cal. Even though she knew he'd rented a cabin near the local campground closest to Mountain Bend, there was always the chance he would come into town to eat or get supplies.

Her odds were much better for meeting him at the club, of course, but could it hurt to hope for a stroke of good luck? Between keeping up with her work and researching a lifestyle that held little to no interest for her other than as a means to an end, the next few days were likely going to fly by.

As soon as she left her room, she smelled the enticing aromas from downstairs and heard the low murmurs of voices. Rounding the bend at the bottom of the stairs took her into the arched entry to the dining room. She recognized Jen Zimmerman, the proprietress, from her photo on their website when Jen looked her way and came toward her with a welcoming smile.

"I heard you made it in with no trouble, Amie. I'm Jen, and that" – she nodded toward a tall man who was standing behind a small, corner bar – "is Drew. Welcome. Would you like me to seat you with someone or by yourself?"

Amie eyed Jen's black dress slacks, white blouse, and paisley vest and grew uncomfortable with her casual attire. "Maybe I should get my bags from the car and change first."

"Nonsense, you're fine. Trust me, I'd be in my jeans if I didn't have to play hostess. Look around. Some come casual, others in their church clothes."

She scanned the diners, noticing Jen was right. "In that case, I would prefer not sitting with strangers this time. I'm still getting my bearings. Thank you."

The hardwood floors gleamed under the white draped tables as she followed Jen to a table by one of the windows, not too far from the long buffet. "Oh my," she mumbled as she caught a glimpse of the offerings steaming under heat lamps and the bread and dessert choices. "I can feel the weight gain already."

Jen laughed, brown eyes crinkling at the corners. "There are plenty of activities to help you work off the calories. As soon as it slows down, I'll come back and tell you more about what's available around here. Help yourself when you're ready. Coffee, tea, and juice are at the beverage bar, and Drew is serving mimosas and Bloody Marys."

Amie nodded then made her way to the food. Picking up a small plate for salads and a larger one for the main courses, she shifted to the back of the buffet row and didn't bother looking up before reaching for the scrambled eggs-and-spinach serving spoon. When her hand landed on top of a wide palm, her startled gaze traveled up the thick forearm sprinkled with dark hair, past a bulging bicep and broad shoulder covered with a worn denim work shirt. She had trouble swallowing past the lump in her throat as she took in a tanned neck, chiseled jaw, and dark-beard-shadowed cheeks before encountering a pair of amused, startling green eyes.

Talk about eye candy. Yum. Heat stole over her face, and Amie gave herself a mental shake, jerking her hand back. "Sorry. I wasn't paying attention."

"No need to apologize."

His deep voice curled her toes, and Amie wondered why in Omaha, with its share of rugged cowboys, she'd never encountered one as instantly compelling as this man.

Turning the spoon handle around, he gave

her a slow, devastating-to-her-libido smile. "Ladies first. I'm Ben, and I'm guessing you're a guest since I don't recognize you."

Cocking her head, she took the spoon and scooped up some eggs. "Amie. Do you know everyone?"

"Just about. One of the perks, and sometimes an annoyance of growing up in small-town America. Don't pass up the hashbrowns," he said when she handed over the serving spoon and took a step forward. "They're from scratch, like everything else."

"Maybe a few, but I have to save room for the apple-cinnamon scones. I fell asleep last night smelling those and drooling." His casual friendliness set her at ease, and she flashed him a smile. Now, if she could get her heart to quit going pitter-patter like she was some lovesick schoolgirl, she might make it down the line without looking and sounding like an idiot.

"Grace outdoes herself every week. How long will you be visiting us?" he asked, piling sausage and bacon on his plate that she eyed with envy. There was only so much room in her stomach, so some things had to be skipped.

"A few days to a few weeks," she replied evasively since she planned to leave as soon as possible. Everything depended on meeting Cal and putting her nonexistent acting skills to work getting something incriminating from him. Just the thought of getting close to the jerk sent shivers down her spine, but all she had to do to dispel them was picture Myla in that rehab.

Ben paused after adding a fried chicken breast to his heaped plate, eyeing her with a potent, curious stare that made her pulse jump and her mouth go dry.

They both moved toward the salad offerings as he asked, "And, during your either short visit or a longer stay, do you have plans lined up?"

Keeping her attention on filling her small plate with tossed greens and fruit, she struggled with how to answer without coming across as rude or suspicious. "I had to take a working vacation, so I'm still looking at what will fit into my schedule." Seeing no way around it, after she added dressing to her tossed salad, she glanced up at him to see his salad plate as crowded as his dinner dish. "I came here because I enjoy the outdoors, and Idaho's tourism websites were irresistible." She felt bad for the lie after he'd been so nice but saw no other choice.

"It's a beautiful area, if you're the outdoorsy type. This time of year, the temperature can go either way."

Was that a touch of skepticism lacing his voice? Before he could say anything else, another tall, rugged cowboy carrying a loaded a plate cast an appreciative look her way. "Sorry I'm late, Ben."

"No problem." Ben nodded toward Amie. "Neil, this is Amie, a visitor for a few days or a few weeks. She's not sure which." His voice held a hint of amusement, but his eyes remained sharp and focused.

"Always a pleasure to meet someone new, especially someone so pretty. Welcome to Mountain Bend, Amie."

Neil's light flirtation was something she wasn't used to from men. They either ignored her or pushed for more than she was willing to give. "Thank you. I just arrived last night, but everyone is friendly." Amie shifted her gaze away from the two men as she moved toward the pan of thick, golden-brown waffles and tried to get her mind out of the gutter.

Neil was as jaw-droppingly good-looking as his friend, but something about Ben made her wish she was the type of woman who went for one-night stands. If she weren't here on a personal quest she needed to stay focused on, she'd consider caving to the temptation to indulge in a vacation fling for the first time. And wouldn't Myla love hearing about that? The thought of her friend's gleeful reaction made her lips quiver. The two of them had taken trips together over the years, and twice Myla had invited someone she'd met to her room, taunting Amie the next morning with how much fun sex with a stranger was.

Amie had been both envious and disconcerted over her friend's behavior, which she thought exciting but dangerous and reckless. Just as conflicting were the images flashing through her mind of her and Ben naked in that fancy four-poster bed upstairs. She'd never before had instant fantasies flit through her head upon exchanging a few words with someone for the first time.

"Here." A scone landed on her plate, and she looked up to catch a small smile teasing the corners of Ben's mouth. "You don't have enough on your plate to sustain you long, and Neil was about to get the last one. Consider it a bribe to tell me what you're thinking that brought about this little grin." He traced a calloused fingertip from one corner of her mouth across her lower lip to the other side, leaving tingles in his wake that spread downward to her nipples.

"Hey, you snooze, you lose." Neil winked

at her, a knowing glint in his eyes. "Can I get you something from the bar, Amie, while you come up with an answer for Ben?"

Something about their polite tones held a commanding edge she found both disconcerting and way too hard to resist. "No, thanks. I'll stick with coffee or juice for now." She needed to keep her wits about her until she was far away from at least Ben, the one who affected her on the deepest level. After that, she'd gladly make a trip to the bar.

Cocking his head, Neil said, "Then I hope to see you around. Enjoy your stay."

Amie held up her plate as she and Ben stepped around the end of the buffet line and came toe to toe. Since there was no way in hell she'd reveal what she'd been thinking about him, she sidestepped answering his probing question. "Thanks. I wouldn't want to miss out on trying Grace's scones after smelling them all night."

If she wasn't mistaken, a flash of disappointment crossed his face before he smoothed out his rugged features and tilted his head enough to send a swath of black hair sliding forward toward the corner of his eye.

"Don't blame you. Nice to meet you, Amie."

"Same here." She watched him join Neil at

a table across the room from hers and blew out a breath as her body temperature returned to normal.

Jen walked up to her with a knowing grin that sent another warm flush over Amie's face. "They're almost as hot as my Drew."

Amie was never shy about admitting to an attraction to Myla, but it surprised her how easy she did so with Jen, someone she didn't know well. "Neil draws eyes and invites second looks, but something about Ben takes my breath away." She gave her a rueful smile. "If only I lived closer or had time for a vacation fling." Now *that* she couldn't believe she said aloud. There must be something wrong with her.

"Some things are worth making time for. Here, let me help you."

Handing Jen her salad plate, Amie realized how much she'd piled on the two dishes. "Good grief," she mumbled, following the proprietress. "What was I thinking?"

Setting her plate down on the table, Jen flashed her a smile. "You weren't thinking. That's what happens when one of them snags your attention."

Curious about the phrase, Amie asked, "One of them?"

Jen looked away with a guilty expression

before switching her gaze back to Amie with a smile. “You know, a smokin’ hot cowboy. They can trip the switch on even eighty year olds.”

“Yeah, you’ve got that right.” She settled onto her seat and nodded toward the empty chair across from her. “Can you join me for a minute?”

“Yeah. It’s slowed down enough. Let me get us a mimosa first. Be right back.”

Eyeing Jen’s smooth, long-legged stroll through the tables and her easy, friendly manner with customers, Amie envied her tall, slender build. At five foot five, her one-hundred-twenty pounds were evenly dispersed, leaving her with a rather boring body. Medium-sized breasts, a waist that was a little too soft, hips that were neither too wide nor too narrow, and a soft, round butt that was on the small size. Put all together, her physical attributes were as boring as she.

She dug into her food, resisting the urge to glance across the room at Ben one more time. Between the deep rumble of his voice, his tall, broad-shouldered frame that dwarfed her, and those compelling, green-eyed stares, he was way out of her league, and she shouldn’t be giving him second, third, and fourth thoughts. The month she’d planned on to find, befriend, and coax Cal Miller into revealing something incriminating was as long as she could be away from home. She had a life in Omaha she wanted to get back to and needed to support her best friend through her recovery.

Jen returned and set a tall glass down in front of Amie then took the chair across from her. "What are your plans this week? Maybe I can suggest something."

This was tricky since her only plan other than keeping up with her accounts was to get online and continue her research into the local club, Spurs, and BDSM, since she already managed to secure a guest pass for Friday night. She wondered how many in the small town knew of the private kink club and how many were members. Since she didn't have the guts to ask, she kept her reply evasive and bland.

Amie waited until she swallowed a bite of the spinach quiche to answer. "Some sightseeing, hiking if I can get onto a guided trip or trail ride. I rode some as a teenager and enjoyed it a lot." Scooping up another forkful, she held it up. "Really good."

"Thanks. It's my mother's recipe. I'll get you some brochures on nearby outfitters." A calculated gleam entered her eyes. "Ben often leads groups up into the mountains for day trips. As a park ranger, he knows the area better than most."

Amie reached for her mimosa and sipped the cold, fruity champagne drink, hoping to dispel the heated rush Jen's last comment caused. "I'm not sure I have the stamina for a day-long hike. I'm used to sitting in front of a computer all day." At her questioning look, Amie added, "I'm a medical billing specialist for numerous clients and have to work while I'm here."

"Got it. Well, if you get ahead and can take the time, his treks are worth the effort for viewing the best scenery around these parts. He goes slow, whether on foot or horseback." She finished off her drink and pushed to her feet. "I'll leave some brochures at the front counter for you. Enjoy your afternoon, Amie."

"Thank you. You, too."

Amie saved the scone for last and picked it up as the corner of her eye caught Ben and Neil rising then walking out. She released a sigh thinking their backsides were as nice to ogle as their faces, wide chests, and loose-limbed strides. Ben snatched a black Stetson off a row of hooks at the entry, put it on, and turned to deliver a piercing stare her way. Tingles raced across her skin as he tugged the brim of his hat down and tipped the edge, wearing a crooked smile that made her heart stutter, before pivoting and leaving.

Ah, if only I had the time and the bravado.

****

Outside, Neil turned to Ben with a smirk. “You’re a tease.”

“Just being friendly to a tourist.” *An attractive newcomer with striking blue-green eyes that reveal some but not enough of her inner thoughts.*

It was what she didn’t show or say he wanted to pull from her.

Neil opened his driver’s side door and leaned an arm on the hood. “Uh-huh.”

Ben ignored the skepticism lacing his friend’s tone and walked to his SUV parked behind Neil. Lifting his hand in a wave, he tossed over his shoulder, “See you at work tomorrow.”

Driving back home, Ben couldn’t stop thinking about Amie. Something about the way she had avoided giving him a direct answer concerning her stay bugged him. He could understand her reluctance to divulge her inner musings when he’d gotten nosy but not her hesitancy when he’d asked about her stay. Why would she avoid answering such a simple, generic question? It had been a long time since he’d given a casual acquaintance a second thought, but his brief encounter with the cute tourist left him intrigued and curious.

The shaggy, layered cut of Amie's chin-length, light-brown hair made it easy for it to fall forward, hiding her face when she bent her head, but those striking eyes could be a dead giveaway if she would keep them on him. Too bad she wasn't here to check out Spurs. If she did and if she was a sexual submissive, he could insist on her attention remaining focused on him.

Since wishful thinking never amounted to anything, he forced himself to think about something else, like the tracking he and Dakota planned that afternoon. So

far, there had been no findings or reports of further hunting cruelty, but he wasn't about to wait to come across another tortured animal before getting out there and trying to find this bastard. He was good at tracking, but Dakota was exceptional. After Ben pulled him aside before leaving Spurs last night and told him about the elk and his suspicions, Dakota hadn't hesitated to offer his skills today.

Ben parked in front of the house and grabbed the takeout box of scraps Jen had given him for the dogs. He liked spoiling them after the poor care they'd gotten from their previous owners. As soon as he stepped inside, they surrounded him with their tails wagging and noses nudging the container filled with sausage, bacon, and eggs.

"Sheba, Shadow, behave," he scolded the two larger dogs as they shoved little Sasha aside. Most of the time the stubby-tailed, short-legged mixed breed held her own with the other two dogs, but when it came to food, the shepherd and lab mix were downright rude. "Come on. Food then outside."

By the time he let the dogs run for an hour while he helped Joaquin, his part-time hired hand, turn the horses, steer, and llamas out to pasture, he had fifteen minutes to saddle his bay, Thunder, load him in the trailer, and set out to meet Dakota. The best known hunting preferences in these parts was the Boise River wildlife management area, close to where he'd come across the elk, which boasted an abundance of wildlife roaming around every season. Ben hoped to visit with hunting parties and ask about anything they'd seen or heard that could help identify this guy, or at least give them something to go on.

A short time later, Ben parked in a lot near Lucky Peak Lake, easily spotting Dakota astride Phantom, his dapple-gray Morgan. The horse was large enough to bear Dakota's six-foot-four build.

He unloaded Thunder, mounted, and rode over to his friend, who executed a smooth turn and pulled alongside him so they could keep going. Dakota wasn't one to waste time.

"What do you think? Head north and make our way back around?" Ben asked him.

"That will work. I know there's a hunting party of four on horseback just up ahead, and two guys on ATVs rode east about ten minutes ago."

"With the number of licenses we're checking out, there will be more. I appreciate your time. This is likely a long shot, but better than sitting around all afternoon doing nothing. I didn't get a chance to ask how Rebecca is doing. Is Poppy enjoying her sister's visit?" The two had just met a few months ago when Poppy's adoptive parents had searched for a familial donor for transplant therapy for Poppy. Both were thrilled to have found a sibling after growing up as an only child.

"So much so they're driving me nuts with their constant chatter."

He might sound irritated, but Ben knew how much he cared about Poppy, how worried Dakota had been when she'd undergone her second bone marrow transplant, fearing another rejection. Rebecca hadn't hesitated to come through for the sister she'd just met.

Without glancing toward him, Ben replied, "Yeah, I do relish coming home to my dogs' greeting and the quiet solitude. Not sure I could adjust to having someone around all the time as easily as you and Shawn and Clayton." That much was true, even if there were times he wouldn't mind company in the evening. He rarely ever invited a woman to stay the night. Only when the memories of his brother plagued him enough to emphasize the loneliness of losing the one person he'd shared a close, special bond with.

"You can do anything easily enough for the right person." Pulling up on his reins, Dakota pointed across the meadow they were traversing. Surrounded by forests with the mountains looming as a backdrop, there were numerous trails to choose from leading into the woods. "That's the direction the group of four took."

"Let's see if we can catch up to them."

It took them a while, but Dakota's talent for tracking had them reaching the hunters in less than thirty minutes. They'd already bagged a good-sized mule deer and were resting alongside a gurgling creek.

"Afternoon, gentlemen. Do you have a few

minutes?" Ben dismounted and flashed his park ranger badge as they strolled toward the men.

A shorter, heavyset guy pushed to his feet and held out his hand in greeting. "Jim Baker. What can we help you with, Ranger?"

Ben asked if they'd come across any maimed wildlife or carcasses they needed to attend to without giving away why they were checking. For all he knew, their sadistic hunter could be one of these guys. "We occasionally get a call about a suffering animal or one a hunter left behind."

All four men frowned, as if disgusted by both possibilities. They were either good actors or innocent of the debauchery. Three shook their heads, mumbling they hadn't seen anything, but Baker scratched his bristled chin with a thoughtful look.

"I can't say I've seen anything, but just the other evening, sittin' around the campfire with about ten others, someone mentioned having to kill a cougar caught in a steel trap that afternoon. I thought he'd planned to take it to the ranger station, or that's what I recall him saying. Maybe mid-fifties, about six foot, but his face was in the shadows."

One of the others nodded and chimed in. "Yeah, I remember that. That's what he said. Sounded pissed about the cat's suffering."

"Okay, thanks, fellas. I'll look into that." Ben fished out a card and handed it to Jim. "Call me direct if you see or hear anything else. Have a good one."

"So, something to follow up on. That's good," Dakota said as they steered their mounts down the creek.

"Any lead is better than nothing." But still not much to go on. Middle age and tall described the majority of licensed hunters.

Chapter Three

"No, I want to, Myla," Amie insisted. Sprawled on her bed Sunday evening, propped up against the pillows, she held the phone to her ear and listened to Myla's continued objections to her staying in Mountain Bend for the next few weeks. "Honestly, it's no bother. I can work until early afternoon then play amateur sleuth around town this week until I go to the club Friday night. From the little I've seen, this is a nice place. You just concentrate on getting better. Besides, you know I'm not the daredevil one between the two of us."

"You don't have...to be. You know as...well as I...how easily you...get yourself into...a jam, and I'm...not there to...get you out of trouble."

Her stalled speech lacked the stuttering of words now, pleasing Amie with her progress. At least she was now trying instead of fighting everyone. "You act like we're still kids, and I'm still a wimp compared to you. You taught me to like pushing myself past my comfort zone, but that doesn't mean I'm reckless. I agree this trip is a long shot, but no more than your visit to the club in Omaha. Myla, I *have* to try, just like you had to try for Mike." Okay, that was probably low, mentioning Mike and the similarity between her need to get justice for Myla and Myla's for her brother. "The club is my best bet, and it's only open on Friday and Saturday, so, until then, I'll hang around town."

Myla's laugh warmed Amie. "Sorry, hon. I... just can't picture...you faking it with those...Doms."

Amie chuckled, agreeing with her. "Since I don't plan on doing anything except watching, it shouldn't be a problem. From what you've said and what I've read, nothing is forced – I won't get kicked out for not participating, right?"

"Correct, but...you'll...get noticed more...the longer you...hold out. I met a few...who were very... persuasive."

The two of them had never gotten a chance to talk about Myla's experience at the club. Between the accident after she'd left that night, her critical condition for weeks, and then her difficulty with talking before Amie left, they'd never brought up the subject. Curiosity and something in her tone prompted Amie to ask about it now.

"Just what did you do the one time you went?"

"Get ready to...fan yourself, girlfriend," she returned with an exaggerated drawl. "There was one I...couldn't say no to. Bondage was...kinda exciting... but I damn...near came from his...light spanking."

"You're kidding, right?" No way could she picture her independent, ball-busting best friend getting turned on from a spanking. "I'm not buying that, Myla."

"Well, it's...true. I never thought...it's hard to explain...just trust me...it stung but...felt good."

That made no sense, but she let it go. She was sure Myla wasn't remembering correctly. From what she'd learned, spanking was a disciplinary act, and sounded awful, especially when administered using an implement. She admitted she'd flushed when her girly parts had tingled as she viewed a video of an over-the-knee hand spanking but figured if she possessed a kinky craving, it would be voyeurism. Given her response during that short video, watching was fun titillation.

"If you say so. Have you seen Matt lately?" she asked, deciding it was time to change the subject.

Myla paused before answering, and Amie wondered what was going on between the two.

"Not since Friday...right after you...stopped by on...your way out. We...he's not...happy with...me. He can't...understand...about Mike."

Sadness had crept into her voice, and Amie suspected she cared more for Matt than she let on but was using his lack of support for her obsession with getting justice for Mike as an excuse to keep him away. "Don't shut him out, Myla. You were growing close before the accident."

"That was...before. Gotta go...they're here...to torture me...again."

Amie injected a note of humor into her voice as she said, "It'll help prepare you if you ever go back to a kink club. Love you – bye." She hung up before Myla could argue.

Knowing her friend well, she suspected Myla was afraid of resuming her relationship with Matt because of her disabling trauma. Given her current limitations, Amie didn't blame her for being cautious moving forward but believed Matt truly cared enough to stand by her through thick and thin. Then again, she'd spent time with him since Myla's accident and had witnessed firsthand his reaction to the news of the car wreck, the extent of her injuries, and the way she'd tried to shut him out ever since. Such grief and worry couldn't be feigned.

There was nothing she could do to mend Myla and Matt's relationship, but she could continue with her plans to seek justice for her and Mike. She showered and read for a while before turning in and wasn't surprised when she fell asleep thinking about a tall, midnight-haired cowboy with striking green eyes and a compelling voice.

Amie descended the staircase the following afternoon, liking the creaks that added to the character of the old inn, and spotted Jen halfway down.

"Where are you off to this afternoon?" Jen asked.

"Playing tourist by looking around for some unique gifts to take home. Any suggestions?" Amie padded over to the counter Jen stood behind.

"If you like to walk, the downtown area is about four blocks from here, and you'll find several gift shops with things from local craftsmen and artists. Here." Jen handed her a map that labeled every store, dining option, and city building along three streets. "There's also a parking lot on the corner across from the library, adjacent to the park."

Taking the information, she smiled. "Thanks. I'll walk since I'll be back before the sun goes down and it turns cool."

"Have a good afternoon. I'm tempted to play hooky and go with you."

"Don't even think about it," Drew said, coming out of a small office down the hall. "If you took off and left me with all this paperwork, I'd be tempted to retaliate."

"You're no fun," Jen returned with an exaggerated sigh and small smile.

Raising a brow, her husband coasted his hand down her back, resting it at the top of her right buttock. Jen fidgeted, Drew's intense stare reminding Amie of Ben.

"There's a time for work and a time for fun. Right, Amie?" Drew flicked her a grin.

"I've always found it best to stay completely out of marital discussions. But, on that note, I've finished my work for the day, so I'm off to have fun." Holding up the town map, she added, "Thanks for this."

Setting out on foot, Amie wondered what it would be like to have someone in her life who could read her every move and communicate with just a look or phrase. As she reached the second block, her thoughts skipped from the Zimmermans to Ben, and she found herself speculating about his relationships, whether he was committed to anyone or still playing the field. She hoped it was the latter as she'd hate to have her fantasy bubble burst if he turned out to be a two-timing jerk like one of her exes.

By the time she reached Main Street, she'd grown frustrated with her lack of willpower to keep from thinking about a man after only one brief encounter. Amie hoped she met him again over the next few weeks so she could prove his impact on her wasn't the strong yearning for some unnamed connection she kept experiencing.

As soon as she came to the library around the corner and saw the name of her favorite romantic suspense author splashed across the front window, advertising an S.L. Anders book signing a week from Friday, all thoughts of Ben flew out of her head. She was currently reading Ms. Anders' newest release and would love to purchase a signed paperback. After making a note on her cell calendar, she found a book at the library, got a temporary card at checkout, then spent the next hour visiting the shops and enjoying the friendliness of the small town.

Amie gave herself an hour to play tourist, purchase a few gifts and souvenirs while keeping an eye out for someone who looked like Cal. By the time she'd made her way down one side of the street and up the opposite side, her stomach was rumbling, and she stepped into the deli for a sandwich. She left biting into a turkey and avocado on whole grain bread, still smiling from Hatti, the owner's exuberant greeting.

She could get used to getting around on foot instead of driving everywhere and eventually knowing everyone around town.

By Wednesday, Amie was kicking herself for arriving in Mountain Bend after Spurs was closed for that week, forcing her to find things to do in the afternoons to keep busy and her mind off what she'd planned. Had she thought it through, she would have arrived late tomorrow, leaving little time to fret over how she would handle her first visit to a private club that held no personal interest for her. Alternative sexual practices aside, she'd outgrown clubbing a few years ago, preferring quieter socializing in smaller groups following the breakup of her one-and-only long-term relationship. Chris had broken her heart when he'd ditched her for someone else, and in the eighteen months since, there hadn't been anyone else. Myla often teased her, reminding her forty was now considered middle age, not thirty, and that she was still young.

As she followed Jen's instructions and her GPS and drove out to River Trails Excursions for the afternoon three-hour hike she'd signed up for this morning, she hoped the long trek would tire her out. She needed the physical exhaustion to override her mental fatigue from the lack of sleep she'd suffered ever since Myla had planted an image in her head of a deep-voiced Dom ordering Amie over his lap. Goose bumps had prickled across her buttocks as she changed into a pair of loose jeans, not from the thought of agreeing to such an order but because the man whose image popped into her head was Ben. The same man she still couldn't quit thinking about since meeting him at the buffet.

Amie blamed that uncharacteristic reaction on her weak, deprived libido then shoved it aside to watch for the turnoff leading to River Trails. She spotted the arched log entrance as she passed a herd of bison grazing with lazy lumbering on the vast rangeland spread out around her. Nebraska's rural areas, miles of farmland, and open ranges were no match for the wide expanse of Idaho's rugged, unspoiled landscape.

A small group was already gathered outside the main building, and Amie parked in the adjacent lot, wasting no time in joining them. Water bottles, binoculars, and bright orange vests were handed out along with instructions from Travis, their guide, to remain close to the group at all times. Amie moved near the end of the line as they started out, making friends with a young newlywed couple, Amber and Dave.

The temperature dropped once they entered the forest and followed a wide, well-worn path through the dense trees. Travis paused to describe foliage and wildlife indigenous to the state, and they stopped at lookout points so everyone could use their binoculars to view the breathtaking scope of the valleys and mountains. Amie caught her breath at the waterfalls at the next point, the rushing cascade of water so powerful, a light mist chilled their faces even from a distance. The air had grown thinner with the slow steady trek upward, but they weren't high enough for the change to matter much.

"I know this is a scenic spot, but we have to keep moving if we're going to get back before dusk," Travis announced just as something, or rather someone snagged Amie's attention through the field glasses.

Leaning against the rail, she went rigid and sucked in a breath. Yes, that was a hunter decked out in camouflage minus the required bright-orange vest for easy detection. He was leaning against a tree, aiming a rifle, so she could only make out part of his profile, and that from a distance, but could swear he resembled Cal Miller. She needed to get closer, though, to be sure.

"Hey, Amie, come on." Amber called her over as the group started out again.

"Coming."

Disappointed, she followed at the rear until they passed another path veering off to the left, the direction she needed to go for a better view of the hunter. Halting, she glanced back, wondering if she had time to take a quick detour. She wasn't worried about losing the group – Travis had said they would follow the same trail up and back. And the next stop was their halfway point where they'd rest, eat snacks, and then start the return hike down. If she hurried, she could dash down that other trail and, if she didn't find a place to have another peek at the hunter, come right back. Even if she took a minute at a lookout spot, it would only take a second to determine if the hunter was Cal.

Before she could chicken out, Amie made sure no one was looking then ran back to the other path. Tiny prickles of apprehension skated over her skin as the trees seemed to close around her along the much-narrower trail. She struggled to breathe as she pushed forward, the closed-in feeling adding to her misgivings. She was about to turn around when the trail ended at an open copse that offered the better, closer view she'd risked this detour for.

Standing with feet braced apart, she looked through the binoculars, searching the same area where she'd seen the hunter. Disappointment swamped her when she couldn't find anyone. The distant report of gunfire prompted her to slip into the woods and take a few more minutes to look.

****

Ben rode Thunder into the meadow where he found Travis and his hikers with no problem after getting the missing person alert. Choosing to ride today instead of drive around his assigned area had placed him nearest to the group, and he now hoped like hell they could find the missing hiker before nightfall. Other rangers were already en route to help. According to Travis, the woman had gone missing somewhere between the falls and Vantage Point, the two spots not that far apart but leaving a lot of woods to comb through.

Travis walked over, worry lining his face and tone as he said, "That was fast. Her name is Amie Buchanon, and the couple in front of her confirm she was right behind them when we left the falls."

The first name brought to mind the young woman Ben had met a few days ago in line at the B&B's buffet. He remembered light-brown, sun-streaked hair in a shaggy cut and a cute smile, but it was her vivid blue-green eyes and evasion in answering what should have been friendly, casual, get-to-know-you topics he couldn't seem to stop recalling.

"Give me a brief description of her and her clothing," he returned, dismounting and doubting it could be the same person until Travis answered.

"Five foot four, brown, neck-length hair, jeans, and a light blue sweatshirt under an orange vest." He waved a hand behind him, indicating the rest of the group wearing the neon safety garment. "You'll know it's her by her eyes – an unusual, bright shade of turquoise."

What are the fucking odds? Ben's first priority was to find Amie. He could take the time later to figure out why a surge of anticipation shot through him when Travis described the same Amie he'd met before.

"I'll retrace your path and go from there. Keep in touch." He pointed to the two-way radio clipped to his waist then took off at a brisk pace down the trail, leaving Thunder with Travis. He could search through the trees easier on foot.

Even though he couldn't deny looking forward to seeing the woman who had occupied his thoughts following their short encounter again, he really hoped her lost status wasn't due to foolishness on her part. He much preferred dealing with land management or wildlife issues as opposed to the consequences of reckless actions by tourists who failed to observe the safety rules.

Ben cupped his hands around his mouth and called out Amie's name loud enough for his voice to echo into the trees. Halfway back to the falls, he was approaching a path that went deep into the woods, one only experienced hikers used, when he heard the fast clomp of running feet, brush rustling, and heavy breathing. He called her name again, rushing forward so fast when he caught a bright-orange flash through the foliage, he almost plowed her down when she came barreling out onto the main trail.

Amie gasped, panting, and Ben grabbed her upper arms to steady her. Her muscles trembled under his palms from her exertions, her face beet red as she looked up with a startled expression.

Those eyes struck him in the solar plexus with the same impact as before, the punch turning his voice rough. "Are you all right, Amie?"

"I...you." She shook her head, and a strand of hair got caught in her mouth. She reached up to tug it aside and only then seemed to realize he held her in a light grip. "Oh dear. Yes, yes, I'm fine. Sorry. You took me by surprise."

"Right back at you. Give me a second here." Releasing one arm, he retrieved his radio and let everyone know he'd found her. She blanched, looking away from him as she realized how fast Travis had discovered her gone and reacted.

As soon as he clicked off, her gaze swung back to him. "Why are you...*oh*." She took in his khaki ranger's shirt and the identifying badges, squirming under his intense observance.

Sliding his hand down to her elbow, he nudged her to fall into step with him as he pivoted. "Yes, I'm a parks-and-wildlife ranger, and, yes, an SOS went out the moment your guide noticed you weren't with the group. You can explain what happened when we get back to them."

Now that he'd found her safe, annoyance crept in to override his relief. She wasn't hurt and didn't appear scared or confused, which pleased him. But that also meant she had some explaining to do. Eyeing her askance while they walked, he could almost see the wheels turning in her head as she chewed on her plump lower lip. Voices from her group filtered through the trees as they neared them, and her steps slowed.

"Maybe you could just escort me back to River Trails."

Hearing the nervous tremor in her voice, Ben almost felt sorry for her. He shook his head, replying, "I'd have to take you up with me on Thunder, and that would be uncomfortable for a city girl." He liked the idea of holding her close more than he was concerned about her comfort, so he might change his mind.

She sent him a questioning glace as they reached the open meadow and the delayed hiking party. "Thunder?"

He nodded toward his horse waiting patiently for his return and fought back a grin when her shoulders slumped even further. "My ride."

Amie surprised him when she threw her shoulders back, a hopeful expression replacing her disappointment. "I've ridden before."

Before he could reply, Travis was there, and Ben released her elbow, leaving her to stand on her own to explain.

"Ms. Buchanon, I'm glad you're okay. You were keeping up with the hike with no problem. What happened?" Travis asked with an edge to his polite tone.

Ben wasn't surprised when she shifted her eyes away from Travis' direct look. "I'm so sorry. I...I stopped to get a stone out of my shoe then got sidetracked when I saw..." She bit her lip again and shrugged. "I'm not sure what it was, an odd looking critter I tried to get a better look at, and I wandered too far. I hurried back as fast as I could." Embarrassment and guilt spread in a blush over her face.

"Getting turned around or losing track of time is easy to do when you're in the woods. I'm afraid our delay means you won't have time to rest as we need to start the return hike. Can you handle that?"

"Yes. I promise I won't hold you up."

Amie's obvious discomfort with the trouble she'd inadvertently caused and the fatigue showing in her bruised look compelled Ben to table his suspicion of her explanation. Travis's face mirrored his skepticism of her story, but they were both professional enough not to call her out on it in front of the others who were all listening with avid interest.

"Why don't I take her back on Thunder," he offered, changing his mind. "She looks tired, and that'll ensure no delays in returning before dark."

Riding back with him might be uncomfortable for Amie, but at least he could spare her the awkward return trek with the group whose outing she'd disturbed. Whether her claim of previous experience on a horse was true or not didn't concern him since he'd be in control of both Thunder and her safety. And he rather enjoyed the idea of controlling her, even though it wasn't in the capacity of a Dom but his job as a ranger.

Relief chased across her face, and her lips curled in a smile of gratitude. "Thanks, I appreciate that."

Travis nodded, appearing relieved. "Let's get going, then."

A few hikers called out goodbye to Amie, which she returned as Ben took her elbow again and led her toward Thunder.

"Thanks again..." she started to say when he turned toward her to help her up.

Unable to resist, he cupped her nape and bent to whisper in her ear. "You lied a few minutes ago to Travis. Don't lie to me if I ask you something." He straightened and gripped her waist, noticing the way her face paled and her eyes conveyed worry followed by a flare of anger. Good. He liked a woman with a little fire in her as long as he didn't have to deal with an inferno of blazing antagonism.

Without giving her a chance to reply, he said, "Ready? Straddle the saddle when I lift you." She didn't weigh much despite the full curves he detected under her loose clothing, and he had no trouble hoisting her onto Thunder's back. She gripped the pommel and swung her leg around, her only hesitation when she chanced a glance down from the stallion's height.

Ben settled behind her, her tense muscles relaxing under the arm he wrapped around her waist. "Easy, hon. I won't let you fall."

"I'm good. He's just a lot bigger up here." Amie reached forward with one arm to stroke Thunder's neck while gripping his forearm with her other hand. "He's a beautiful horse."

"Don't tell him that. It'll go to his head." He tilted his head to return the grin she twisted her face around to give him. If she harbored any guilt over her obvious evasions about getting lost, she now hid it well.

With a tug on the reins, he turned Thunder, intending to ride back across the open rangeland skirting the forests and mountain trails. Mileage wise, it was longer, but they could ride faster and would likely beat the group on the return trip. Amie was a comfortable weight against his chest and thighs, her hands soft where she held his forearm below his rolled-up sleeve, and her round buttocks pressed against his groin, a temptation difficult to ignore. He never dallied with tourists, didn't take them out and, given his sexual preferences, never slept with them. But he'd never met someone who had drawn his interest at first sight, whose evasiveness poked at him to uncover her secrets, or whose eyes could shred a man's good intentions with one glimmering flicker.

"Tell me, Amie, have you decided on how long you'll vacation around here?" he asked, kicking Thunder into a trot.

"Oh!" She tightened her grip on his arm with the sudden increase in speed but rallied fast. "Not yet. I'm winging it."

"Kind of like you did when you went chasing after that odd-looking critter? Did you ever get close enough to make out what it was?" Ben tucked the reins into his other hand without loosening his arm around her waist and pulled his hat lower to ensure it stayed on during the vigorous pace.

"No, I never saw it again."

Convenient. He shouldn't bother with her or

care why she was so secretive. She, and her reasons, were none of his business. But he couldn't ignore how often his thoughts over the past three days had strayed toward their initial introduction and his reaction to hearing about her going missing then seeing her again. Attraction and lust were separate from those responses and much easier to disregard and walk away from.

"While you're here, I can make time to take you on another trail hike or a riding excursion on your own mount. When it comes to Idaho wildlife, I'm an expert."

She was quiet for so long, he slowed Thunder and peered down at her. "Still with me?"

"Yes, sorry. I'd like that if I can get the time."

"You have a tendency to apologize a lot, even when it's unnecessary. You don't need to with me. Hold on, and we'll let Thunder stretch his legs."

He clutched her closer as her hands squeezed his arm, then he kicked the stallion into high gear. Thunder didn't hesitate, bolting across the vast, open terrain at a ground-eating run. Amie's squealing laughter echoed in the air, amusing Ben with her exuberance and lack of anxiety. She either trusted him or possessed a daredevil streak. Either one worked for him.

As Ben predicted, they reached the River Trails excursion post before the hikers. The three of them were breathing heavy when he reined Thunder in, slowing him to a walk the last quarter mile. Halting at the corral, he swung down then reached up and plucked her from the saddle. It wasn't he who pulled her close but all Amie's doing closing the gap between them.

Not that he was complaining. He was a guy, and, despite his issues with her vague replies to simple, nonpersonal inquiries and outright fabrication of the circumstances regarding her earlier disappearance, he could admit those soft curves stirred his blood.

Amie released a rush of air, as if she'd been holding her breath. "That was a blast. Thank you."

Fighting the temptation to pinch her chin and hold her still for a heavy assault on those soft lips, he offered her a slow smile and friendly nod and released her. "You're welcome." He pulled a card from his shirt pocket, handed it to her, and tipped his hat. "Call me if you want that private trail ride. Try not to get lost again." Taking the reins, he pivoted and strode toward his truck and horse trailer without glancing back.

Chapter Four

Amie gave herself a mental kick for standing there ogling Ben's broad shoulders, nice backside, and sexy, long-legged stride across the parking lot. She was still working at catching her breath from that wild, vigorous ride, but it was his snug hold of her against his rock-hard body that left her vibrating with pleasure. Her blood heated as she recalled the strength of his ripped arm around her waist, his wide, thick chest against her back, and his thigh muscles contracting under her. At first, she'd found sitting with her butt constantly shifting against his groin an embarrassing distraction, but the excitement of his closeness and the ride soon took over.

Her gratitude for the return ride that spared Amie an uncomfortable trek back with the group helped her deal with the guilt and mortification from the trouble her actions had wrought. At least she had the comfort of confirming Cal Miller was in the area to excuse her actions, even if she couldn't reveal that tidbit to anyone. She'd spotted him not far from her first sighting and with a closer, clearer look, she was sure of his identity. That one glimpse had shaken her, knowing what he was capable of.

Hurrying to her car, Amie slid behind the wheel, wanting to leave before the others returned, wanting to spare herself any further awkwardness in front of them. She needed to set aside her chagrin over the consequences she hadn't foreseen when she'd slipped away from the group and concentrate on how she would befriend Cal at the club, if he were there. Given her reaction from a distant glance, the task she'd set out to accomplish seemed daunting, the odds of success unlikely.

After picking up a hamburger, she was so hungry, she parked and ate before returning to the B&B. It frustrated her but didn't surprise her when thoughts of Ben kept intruding. Of the several trips she'd taken since college, why did she have to meet someone on this one who jump-started her hormones to the point she couldn't think straight? As much as a short-term affair tempted her, the purpose of her trip remained the same. Amie had yet to figure out how she would fake her way through getting to know Cal. There was no way she could stretch her nonexistent acting skills into including Ben in her deception, not to mention the constant distraction of skin-to-skin pleasurable contact.

But she really wanted to try.

Just imagining it caused her nipples to pucker and her pussy to dampen. Blaming it on her latent libido, she drove back to the inn and spent the evening reading more on private BDSM clubs. She fell asleep picturing herself bound, teased, and sexually tormented by first a stranger with no name or face who was then replaced with Ben's rugged, dark-shadowed image.

Not even in sleep could she escape her infatuation and lust.

Come Friday evening, Amie decided if she couldn't go through with her plan to cozy up to Cal as a friend, she would forget the whole thing and go home. The stress of getting close to him combined with the poor timing of her reawakened interest in men was too much to handle. Myla would understand. In fact, she

kept encouraging her to give up on the idea. The decision would be easier if Myla's struggling-speech pattern didn't tug at Amie's heartstrings every day, and hearing about the hardships of her physical therapy didn't depress her as much they did

Myla.

Other than Grace's oldest daughter staffing the front desk, no one else was around as Amie came downstairs, sparing her from coming up with a lie about her plans for the evening. She didn't need more tension added to nerves already stretched taut as a bowstring. Given the way she'd squirmed in her chair while researching, and how her blood heated when she'd read or viewed certain scenes, her first visit to a private club might end up as the only positive from her plan. If so, and all else failed, Myla would at least get a kick out of Amie's adventure tonight.

"Have a nice evening," was all the girl said when Amie sent her a wave.

"You, too."

Walking around to the rear parking area for guests, she pulled her knee-length sweater wrap around her, shivering from the brisk, cold breeze. It turned damned-near frigid around here with a night wind, or maybe she wasn't used to going out with bare legs under a skirt this time of year. Her guest pass stated she could wear whatever she chose on the first night, but she'd decided on something in between slacks and the required-for-members lingerie or skimpy outfits revealing a lot of skin.

She'd paired the plain black skirt that flared around her mid-thighs with a sleeveless turquoise blouse, hoping the club was kept warm to accommodate those wearing next to nothing, or nothing at all.

Twenty minutes later, Amie found a space in the crowded parking area in front of the two-story log structure and parked. The well-lit entrance revealed the sign Spurs above the double-door entrance, leaving no doubt about the accuracy of the directions on the website and emailed to her. She checked the time and got out, nervous agitation vying for supremacy with titillating anticipation as she pulled one heavy door open and stepped inside a large foyer. A young woman was waiting to greet her and escort her inside.

Padding toward her with a welcoming smile and outstretched hand, the attractive blonde said, "Amie? I'm Lisa. My fiancé, Master Shawn, is one of the owners of Spurs."

Amie pressed her hand. "Nice to meet you, Lisa. I love your dress."

The top half of the thin-strapped sheath with scooped neckline was attached to the snug, short skirt with delicate chains in front, on the sides, and, as she turned sideways, also visible in the back.

"Thank you. There's a great boutique in Boise

where we shop. You can hang your wrap in the closet. Since it's your first time, shoes are optional."

"I'm fine leaving my shoes out here." Given the vast difference in their attire, Amie didn't want to draw any more attention to herself as an inexperienced newbie. She shrugged out of her long sweater then toed off her pumps.

Lisa pointed to a row of cubbies along the wall. "Pick an empty one. Your Dom guide and instructor for the evening is busy right now and asked me to get you a drink and start your tour, if that's okay with you."

"Of course," she replied, stowing her shoes. "As long as I'm not keeping you from anything and you don't mind."

"Not at all. Shawn was delayed at work with an arrest and asked me to ride out tonight with our friends so I could be here for you. Ready?"

"I think so." That was about as honest as she could muster. Following Lisa into the massive club, she asked, "Arrest? Is he in law enforcement?"

A proud smile lit up her green eyes. "Yes, he's the sheriff. Do you want to get one of your alcohol drinks now or something else? The bar is over there."

Between hearing one of the owners was a cop who probably wouldn't be too keen on her reason for visiting his club and ogling the activities going on, answering her was easy. “I’ll go for alcohol now.”

Lisa’s eyes twinkled with her light laugh. “Been there, so I get it. Come on. Any questions, don’t hesitate to ask.”

“I don’t know where to begin,” she admitted as they crossed the hardwood floor, her gaze landing on the people dancing to a low, edgy beat at the far end of the room. A few women were topless or their attire hung open, their breasts swaying along with their undulating bodies.

The nudity didn’t shock Amie – that she expected. But as they paused by a woman strapped facedown on a bench with her hips elevated, her buttocks striped with bright-red lines, the look of contentment reflected on the younger girl’s face took her by surprise. Why wasn’t she tense and grimacing from the discomfort?

“Is this our guest for the evening, Lisa?” The man gripping a thin bamboo cane caressed the girl’s abused cheeks.

“Master Simon, this is Amie.”

He nodded in a friendly gesture, but the assessing look in his dark-brown eyes rose goose bumps along Amie’s arms. He winked then pinched the puffy lines marring the girl’s flesh hard enough to draw a low moan from her. “Welcome to Spurs, Amie. Enjoy your visit, and your stay in Mountain Bend.”

“Thank you, Sir,” she replied, remembering the rules. As they continued toward the bar, Master Simon snapped the cane between the bound girl’s legs. She shrieked, and Amie shuddered, planning to stay clear of that Dom.

“Don’t worry,” Lisa said, sliding onto a stool at the bar. “Master Simon is strict and likes the subs into harsher pain, but your Dom isn’t so rigid.”

“Was I that obvious?” she sighed. She’d hoped her extensive research would keep her from standing out as naïve and inexperienced.

“Yes, but don’t let it bother you. We’ve all been there at one time or another. Besides, as a first-time guest and new to the lifestyle, you’ll get to slide on most of the rules, and I’m sure you read you have control over what you want to try, if anything.”

“How about with whom?” Eyeing the tall blond bartender coming their way when they settled on two barstools, Amie thought she wouldn’t mind getting to know this man.

“Not so much choice there, as your guide has already been chosen for tonight and this one” – Lisa smiled at him – “is already spoken for. Isn’t that right, Master Clayton?"

"That would be correct, Lisa. You must be Amie. Welcome. What can I get you two?"

Amie returned his grin, Master Clayton's obvious satisfaction with his relationship a refreshing change from the committed men she recalled hitting on her at college parties and later at clubs. "A whiskey and Coke, please."

She took a moment to scan the people at the bar while Lisa gave him her order, but none of them were Cal Miller. Turning her attention back to Lisa, she asked, "So, who is my instructor tonight, and what can you tell me about him?" She was anxious to look for Miller, and she couldn't do that sitting at the bar.

"He asked me to let him introduce himself, but I can say you won't be disappointed. He's a good Dom, strict but fair, like most. If you don't leave tonight wanting more from him, there's something seriously wrong with you," Lisa teased.

Funny, Amie mused, that was her exact thought about Ben. "There doesn't seem to be a shortage of eye-catching men around here." And since there weren't, maybe this guy would be the distraction she needed to put Ben out of her mind so she could focus on her goal of getting justice for Myla.

"That's true, but that just means there are more of the guys you'll want to stay clear of as well as those worth getting to know." Lisa turned her head toward the stairs and smiled as Clayton returned with their drinks. "Speaking of which, two of them are headed this way."

"I don't think Master Shawn would like that gleam in your pretty eyes, Lisa," Clayton warned with a raised brow.

Lisa's reply went unheard by Amie as she made the mistake of sipping her drink while following Lisa's gaze. She choked and coughed seeing Ben and Neil coming their way before Neil veered toward the back, her eyes watering after their unexpected appearance took her by surprise.

Shit and double damn. I'm so screwed.

Clayton reached across the bar and tapped between her shoulders. "You okay?" he drawled with a hint of humor in his voice.

Nodding, she replied with a wheeze. "Yes, thanks." Her face grew warm when Ben stood before her, appearing nonchalant at seeing her here.

"I appreciate you keeping Ms. Buchanon company for me, Lisa. Thanks," he told Clayton as he handed him a beer.

"No problem. I enjoyed meeting you, Amie,"

Lisa said. "Have fun tonight."

"Thanks, you, too, Lisa," she managed despite her pounding heartbeat.

Thankfully, Ben defused the awkward situation by gripping her elbow and helping her off the stool. Leaning against his big, rock-hard body again sent a wave of heat through her veins, her pulse leaping with an expectation she couldn't control.

"Let's go sit over here," he instructed.

It took every ounce of effort on Amie's part not to stumble on her shaky legs as she went with him to an empty table. He returned greetings from other members without breaking his stride and didn't release her until he held out a chair for her.

"Have a seat, and we'll talk."

Since he'd taken his hat off, she could see his face and eyes clearly, yet couldn't read anything from his bland expression. Not trusting her voice, she sat down and dared several sips of her drink, hoping the booze would soothe her jangled nerves. In all the times thoughts of him had intruded in the past five days or during their ride, she'd never considered he might have a membership here. Thinking back and seeing him in this sex-charged atmosphere, his presence shouldn't have shocked her. Those sharp eyes and the dominant control he'd exerted in small, concerned ways should have clued her in.

As soon as he took the chair next to her, she blurted, “You told Lisa to keep your name from me on purpose. Why?”

“After I was given your name earlier, I wanted to observe your honest reaction. I didn’t know before tonight you were our guest, in case that was your next question. My turn. Why are you here, Amie?”

Before she could stop herself, she shifted her gaze over his shoulder, trying to avoid his astute observation. Which was dumb since his next demand proved that same keen attention also caught her subtle move.

“Look at me when we talk, Amie.”

Huffing a frustrated breath, she faced him and tried her best to sound convincing by giving him part of the truth. “My interest was piqued when my best friend visited a club back home and told me about her experience. We were supposed to make this trip together, but she was injured in a car accident and had to cancel.”

Ben took a swig of beer, his eyes never leaving her face, and she was too distracted by the movement of his thick, tanned throat as he drank, to guess if he believed her. She imagined most people visiting for the first time got caught up in the eye-popping scenes taking place around the room, like the couple fucking on the hay bales stacked against the wall opposite the bar. Her quick peek over Ben's shoulder landed on Neil a few tables over, a brunette kneeling between his spread knees, her mouth working his cock. But neither erotic scene fazed her as much as one intense, green-eyed look from Ben or the slightest press of his warm, muscled body against hers.

So not good.

"You traveled alone and stuck with your plan to visit us without your friend along? I could point how unwise it is for a young woman to travel by herself, but, given your independent nature, I won't waste my breath." He nodded toward her almost-empty glass. "Finish your drink, and we'll see how far your interest goes."

Going by the images running through her mind, there was no telling where this would lead with him as her Dom. Downing the last swallow, she contemplated the merits of killing two birds with one stone by continuing to search for Cal while giving in to her lust for Ben and going for a vacation fling. The only problem she could see with that plan was her ability to fit in here and submit to his dominant demands. Getting excited by watching was a far cry from participating.

Amie decided she wouldn't know until she tried. Sucking in a deep breath, she lowered the glass and pushed to her feet. "Okay. I'm ready."

****

Somehow, Ben doubted that, but he rose, and, this time, chose the more intimate touch of taking Amie's hand instead of her elbow. He had asked Lisa to visit with her first to give him time to observe her reaction to the club. When he'd first learned the name of tonight's guest, a jolt of expectant pleasure had shot through him, and he'd had no trouble imagining which scenes he would enjoy introducing her to the lifestyle with. Although he'd wanted to see Amie again, he'd never imagined it would be here at Spurs. After observing her with Lisa and noticing the way she appeared more interested in searching for someone than with the activities in play, his suspicions about her motive for coming tonight kicked in. That didn't keep him from wanting her any more than her evasive story when she'd been separated from the hiking group.

He had to keep reminding himself they were just acquaintances, not in any kind of relationship either here or outside of these walls. That meant he could only insist on so much with regard to her private thoughts. Acting as her guide tonight didn't give him the right to demand she reveal every personal tidbit about her life, only those thoughts pertaining to her interest in their lifestyle. That didn't mean he would tolerate outright lies, and he needed to establish that hard line before they got started.

Drawing her up against his side with a tug of her hand, he lifted his free hand to place his knuckles under her chin and nudge her head up. "Honesty is key in any relationship, and especially here, where an evasive or dishonest response could cause emotional or physical harm. When I ask you a direct question tonight, do not lie, Amie. You can tell me you prefer not to answer, and I'll deal with that accordingly, depending on what I need to know."

"I understand, but I did state in my application I'm only interested in observing."

He cocked his head, reading more in those expressive eyes and the way she kept close to him than she was admitting. "Yes, I read that, but you filled that out without knowing me yet, or that I'd be here tonight. Let's not kid each other." Pivoting, he started toward the bondage stations. "There's mutual interest between us, and has been from our first encounter last Sunday. If either of us doesn't want to pursue that in the next hour or two, then we'll part ways. Although, I'll be inclined to think there's something wrong with one or both of us if that's the case." A small smile tilted her mouth at the corners, prompting him to ask simply, "What?"

With a direct look, she replied, "Lisa said something similar."

He squeezed her hand, approval for the honest answer. "Well, she should know. Feel free to ask me anything, and mention if something appeals to you. Do not speak to anyone engaged in a scene without permission. Otherwise, we'll stroll around slowly, and I'll let you get your fill of observing." Keeping conversation between them to a minimum would enable him to concentrate on her reactions. He could learn as much from expressions as from verbal feedback.

Ben noted a lot about Amie in the next twenty minutes. Her face flushed, and her nipples puckered under the silk blouse when they stopped at the first chain station and eyed Skye, Clayton's new girl, relishing each stroke of his multi-strand flogger. That told him Amie wasn't put off by light pain.

Her brows dipped in a frown when they approached the St. Matt's Cross where Neil had Kathie, one of their more adventurous subs, bound.

"Something bothering you about this station?" he asked.

He fought back a wide smile when she went up on her toes and whispered in his ear. "He was getting a blowjob from someone else a few minutes ago."

Neil released Kathie's nipple and glanced their way, his eyes narrowing when he caught Ben's smirk. "What?"

"Our guest is wondering about your switch in subs."

Neil shrugged. "Easy enough, little one. Trish enjoys several Doms, and I don't mind trading partners. It's nice to see you again. Have fun."

With pink-tinged cheeks, she mumbled, "Thank you."

Ben ushered her forward, letting her absorb that as he led her to the new bondage chair, catching the constant shift of her gaze more toward people than the apparatus. The way she would subject certain males, subs, and Doms, to a closer scrutiny was curious but harmless. Her reaction to approaching the sub bound on the bondage chair with her arms strapped on the armrests, her legs restrained apart, and her pussy and anus stuffed with a double vibrator was as telltale as amusing. Her palm turned sweaty, and she bit her lower lip before muttering, "Uh, uh."

“Good enough.” He drew her away and halted at the glass doors leading to the back deck and hot tub before asking, “What about that bothered you?”

Amie didn’t answer at first, her attention snared by Poppy and Dakota enjoying the hot tub. Lying over Dakota’s lap with her shoulders and head elevated braced on her elbows, the redhead grimaced as Dakota lifted one leg to raise her ass out of the water to deliver a resounding swat. Sidling closer to Ben, Amie’s rapt attention and curled toes gave away her interest.

“We’ll get back to the bondage chair. You’re interested in spanking, and what you can get from it other than a bruising punishment. Watch. Poppy loves long sessions over Dakota’s lap, as does Lisa with Shawn.”

Her eyes flew up to his. “I just like watching.”

“Are you sure? I warned you about lying.” Staring at her face, he ran a finger down her chest, dipping under the buttons and her silky bra to trace her soft flesh, stopping just shy of touching her nipple. It took only seconds for her frustration with the light touch and avoidance of her sensitive, puckered tip to darken her vivid eyes and cause her to fidget. “Want to try another answer?”

“Fine,” she snapped out, making no move to

dislodge his finger despite her obvious annoyance with him and the subject. "It interests me."

"That would have been better without the attitude. After tonight, you'll need to curb that. Now, back to the bondage chair." As much as he enjoyed her soft skin, he removed his finger to give her verbal responses his full attention.

Looking over at the contraption, she studied it from a distance with less dislike. "I think it's the exposing pose in public. It's too embarrassing."

"Very good, Amie." Ben resumed walking, heading to the opposite side of the room. "Public exposure is hard for some, easy for others. Add in the vulnerability of restraints and such revealing poses can take getting used to, something any Dom worth his salt will consider."

"But still might insist, right?"

"If you're wondering if I will insist, let's just say I'd love to see you restrained in various positions, open and willing to please me. When I think you're ready and can handle it. This is my favorite bench." The plain padded spanking bench offered the option of cranking the end high enough to place the sub in a head-down, hips-at-the-perfect-height-for-fucking position. "And look, it's available. Are you brave enough for a mild demonstration?"

She fidgeted, bit her lower lip again, but there was no denying the flush of excitement covering her neck and face and the flare of old-fashioned lust in the look she gave him. “Clothes on?”

He nodded, disappointed but expecting that. “Yes, unless you agree otherwise at some point. You know the safe words, right?”

“Yes, red for stop, yellow to pause, green I’m good to keep going. What if I want less, or more?”

“You’re free to talk, so let me know.” Two men stepped up to the chain station a few feet from them, and Ben didn’t miss the way her gaze swung toward them, or how she studied them as if discerning if she’d seen them before as Master Chase bound his long-time sub, Evan. “Curious, or do you recognize them?”

“What? Oh.” Flustered, she tried averting her face, but he grabbed her chin and held her still.

“Look at me when you answer.” He could tell she didn’t want to and had to work at stifling a retort. Too bad.

“Curious,” she said, leaving it at that.

Ben was starting to think Amie had a hidden agenda in coming here, but for now, he’d table his suspicions. Tonight could very well be their last encounter, and if so, her secrets wouldn’t matter.

"Okay. Lie facedown, hips on the edge. I'll only restrain one arm and one leg since this is a first for you."

****

Unable to resist the chance to feel Ben's hands on her while at the same time appeasing her curiosity, Amie caved to the need coursing through her in a hot lava flow of lust. There had been no sign of Cal anywhere in this room. As disappointing as that was, she might as well get something out of this night. At least she wouldn't return home with nothing. She bent over the bench, kneeling on the lower pad, the public venue adding a thrill and uplift to the bravado she needed. She had trusted Ben the park ranger, which boosted her faith in Master Ben enough to dip her toes into this lifestyle. All of her assertions kink held no appeal for her went out the window as soon as she'd imagined herself in some of those scenes they'd watched with Master Ben being the one to torment her body and senses.

Laying her head facedown in the headrest, she held her breath as he wrapped a strap around her right wrist and another just below her elbow.

"Breathe, Amie." The amusement in his tone had her gritting her teeth until he trailed his hand up to her shoulder, down her spine then over her buttock on his way to her legs. The light touch drew warm pulsations, leaving her to wonder what her reaction would be without the barrier of clothes. Moving to her left, he bound her calf then ghosted his fingers up her bare thigh saying, “I like touching your smooth, soft skin. Do you like my hand on you?”

“Yes.” *A lot*. It was easy to admit that when she wasn’t facing him, or anyone else. She couldn’t see if others were watching, which helped, but the music, low voices, and the occasional telltale snap against bare skin followed by a shrill cry or low moan ensured she didn’t forget where they were.

“Good.”

He removed his hand, and she couldn’t help lifting her head to complain. “If my answer was so good, why did you stop?”

“To do this.”

The smack startled her into jumping, the slight sting robbing her of breath until it dwindled to a dull, warm throb. To take her mind off the matching pulse in her pussy, she tested the bonds, which was a mistake. Her inability to move one leg and arm sent another frisson of heat to her elevated crotch, and she prayed her damp panties weren’t showing.

Ben squeezed the spanked cheek then swatted

her other buttock. "If you want me to continue, give me the color."

Amie wasn't about to back out now, not after coming this far and with all the possibilities swimming in her head, not to mention her wet, heated response to those smacks. "Green, please."

"You please me, Amie," he replied, satisfaction lacing his voice.

Amie got as much startling pleasure from his words as she did the volley of smacks that followed. A slow burn built across her backside with each skin-snapping swat, the twinge of pain morphing into a numb drumming. She gasped as he kept up a steady barrage, delivering each spank with the same tempered force – not too light, but not too hard – until she found herself squirming for more of the heated pleasure fueling her arousal. All of her senses zeroed in on her butt, the pleasure/pain both surprising and as disconcerting as it was unexpected. When he halted with an abruptness that jarred her as much as the pulsing heat encompassing her backside, her breath rushed out of her lungs on a *whoosh.*

Ben placed a hard hand on her lower back and pressed, stilling her restless twitching and calming her breathing. "I can't read your mind, Amie, and it's too soon for me to decipher what your body is telling me. Do you want to stop, want more, or less?"

Damn, this honesty crap could be embarrassing. Still, if she wanted to reap as much as possible from this one encounter, why not push her comfort level just a little? "More, please."

The warmth of his big body as he leaned over her eased her shivers of uncertainty; his hot breath in her ear and calloused palm sliding up under her skirt along her thigh sent her pulse skyrocketing.

"How much more?" He palmed one aching buttock over her silk panties, the more intimate touch so much hotter than over her skirt. "Enough to brave a harder touch against this much-thinner barrier?"

Turning her head brought her almost mouth to mouth with his face, the lustful heat in his green eyes making the decision for her. "Yes," she whispered, wishing he would kiss her.

Instead, his wicked grin caused her heart to somersault and, when he bit her earlobe and his deep voice rumbled, "That's my girl," that somersault turned into a flip.

Chapter Five

Voices and movement from those nearest to Amie and Ben became more pronounced as he lifted her skirt, heightening her awareness of both her surroundings and the exposure of her panty-covered butt. But neither prompted her to say red. Just the opposite, in fact. The casual sweep of Ben's hand across her cheeks left a trail of heat and drew a low moan from her. Missing his touch as soon as he removed his hand, she then braced for a harder connection.

The smack landed with more force, delivered more discomfort and heat, a much-sharper sting that stole the air she just inhaled. Before he noticed and told her to breathe again in that amused tone, she sucked in a breath and shook from the next blow. Man, that stung, but *wow*, in such a good, unexpected way.

Ben soothed the ache with a caress, and her

muscles went lax, loving the sensation. "Are you good, Amie?"

"Oh, yeah," she breathed on a soft sigh, arching into his hand. His answering chuckle curled her toes.

"Excellent. Deep breath."

She barely had time to fill her lungs before he let loose with a barrage of resonating, harder smacks that turned her backside into a throbbing mass of fire. With shuddering grunts and escalating arousal that dampened and swelled in her pussy, she accepted each blow, determined to see this through.

Once again, he ceased his torment without warning, but it was the way he struck up a casual conversation with someone she knew while soothing her sore butt that threw her into an emotional tailspin.

"Drew, where's your lovely wife?"

"Visiting with Poppy while I decide where and how I want to torment her tonight. I see it didn't take you long to introduce our guest to a scene."

"In case you don't recognize her," Ben returned with a hint of humor, "Amie is one of your guests also."

She heard footsteps then saw Drew's amused face peering sideways at her as she lifted and turned her head. "It is you. Welcome to Spurs, hon." He winked then moved out of her sightline.

Amie couldn't help wiggling in mortification, imagining Drew's eyes on her. Her white panties were not only skimpy but sheer. Ben put pressure on her buttock, enough to warn her he expected her to remain still. Not wanting a public reprimand, she went rigid and bit her lip to make sure she didn't embarrass him in front of the other man by complaining. Besides, despite the audience, she was enjoying his touch too much to risk losing it.

"Speaking of newcomers," Ben said, sliding his hand down her thigh, "we're on the lookout for a sadistic bastard who would rather maim and leave an animal to suffer than shoot to kill for the meat and hides. Keep an eye out, would you, or let me know if you hear any talk?"

"You bet. I hate fuckers like that. I'll contact you directly. I better go find Jen. Catch you later. Maybe the four of us can get together while Amie is here."

Ben surprised her when he answered, "We'd like that," instead of denying their relationship went any further than this one scene.

Then he unstrapped her arm and leg, and disappointment swamped her as he helped her stand. Unable to help herself, she leaned against him, loving his size and thick arms coming around her.

"Take a moment to get your bearings and steady yourself. I'm proud of you, Amie. You did better than I thought you would."

Frowning, she looked up at him. "You thought I'd back out, didn't you?" she asked, her voice dripping with accusation.

"Yes, I did. What, if anything, do you want to see or do next?"

She didn't understand why his reply bothered her, but she chalked it up to one of the oddities about her reactions to everything tonight. Needing to assimilate it all, especially the burning arousal from the discomfort of her first spanking, she pulled away from his hold and the contentment of his embrace.

"Sorry, but I think I'm ready to call it a night. Thank you for your time."

"In that case, I'll walk you out. Quit apologizing for honest replies."

"I'll try." Myla was always telling her the same thing, but it was a habit she'd picked up as a kid always wanting to please others and had failed to break in all these years.

Pleased he seemed as reluctant to part company as she was, she took the hand he held out and went with him to the foyer. He helped her slip her shoes on, a first for Amie, then held her sweater wrap for her to put on. The night had turned even colder, and she huddled close to him as they walked to her car, reluctant to give up his body heat.

"And here I thought Nebraska was nippy this time of year."

Ben reached for her door handle. "Is that where you're from?"

"Yep, born and raised in Omaha. How about you?"

He looked down at her and unleashed one of those devastating grins. "Born and raised here." Opening her car door, he paused then cupped her nape and hauled her against him before she realized his intent.

As soon as Ben's lips took hers in a deep, tongue-probing kiss, Amie melted against him, loving the way he held her head immobile for his assault. His control stole her breath, and the slide of his mouth over hers, his tongue stroking hers robbed her of coherent thought. But that was okay. He could have both and anything else he wanted as long as he didn't stop. A moan slid from her mouth into his, and he tightened his hand on her neck, drawing her even closer, and a shudder of pleasure racked her entire body.

God, the man can kiss.

Too bad all good things had to come to an end. He released her, and she shivered from the loss of contact, the breeze sending prickly tingles across her damp lips as he ushered her into the car before she grew too chilled. Leaning inside, he surprised her with an invitation she couldn't refuse.

"I'm guiding a trail ride tomorrow. Lunch is provided, and the cost is on me. Can you join us?"

She agreed with unwise enthusiasm but was powerless to say no. "Yes, thanks."

Amusement brought out the tiny lines around his eyes. Pulling out his phone, he said, "Give me your number, and I'll text you directions to the stables where we're meeting."

Amie returned to the inn wondering if she was making a mistake by starting something with Ben. His insistence on honesty posed a problem since she doubted he would agree with her reason for this vacation. Heck, she wasn't even sure *she* agreed with the plan, only that she needed to try something to help Myla.

None of that reasoning kept her from arriving on time for Ben's trail ride the next day.

****

Ben needed something else to think about today besides his parents' call first thing this morning and admitted to that ulterior motive when he'd invited Amie on today's ride. They spoke every week, but he knew they would spend the majority of their conversation this morning asking him how he was coping. They fretted over his grief as much from worrying about his peace of mind as their own in dealing with the death of their child. He hurt for them, but nothing he ever said this time of year convinced them he was fine.

He missed Bart, and always would, but it was the guilt for not being there he continued to struggle with. Providing a home for rescued animals helped fill the void and make amends for failing his brother, but the loss of their special bond still cut deep. His encounters with Amie this past week had provided an unexpected and welcome reprieve from his grief and guilt, prompting his invitation for her to join them today.

Riding single file along the narrow mountain trail, Ben would pause when he spotted a bear, moose, or mountain goats he could point out to the group of five. Amie's expressive face would reveal awe or pleasure, and when he stopped at a mountainside waterfall that poured into a lake in the valley, he couldn't resist getting close to her again.

"This is a good spot to stop for lunch and pictures," he announced, dismounting in the small clearing. Turning to the small group, he avoided showing favoritism by signaling out Amie as he spoke. "Feel free to take your meal over to the picnic table and make use of the telescopes along the rail. We'll hang out here for about thirty minutes."

It was easy to maneuver himself to sit next to Amie at the table when the two couples took their seats side by side. "Are you holding up?" he asked her, hoping she caught on he wanted to know if there were any lingering side effects from his swats last night. "Saddles can chafe after a while if you're not used to riding."

"I'm good, and I'm enjoying the ride even more than the hike I took the other day. The mountains are so beautiful. Thanks for inviting me." Her smile held a wealth of appreciation.

"You're welcome."

Ben turned his attention toward the others and regaled everyone with stories of Idaho's history. After they ate, he escorted Amie over to one of the four telescopes and settled her in front of the long, magnifying lens. With the others still at the table, he pressed against her back, enjoying her soft buttocks cushioning his groin as he clasped her hips.

Bending his head to whisper in her ear, he said, "You feel good. Take a look. The view is spectacular."

She released a trembling breath that matched her quivering muscles. "So do you." Peering through the scope, her tone revealed her wonder at the natural landscape. "Oh, it's beautiful."

He wished she were as openly expressive about everything. No other woman of such short acquaintance had caused such a need in him to learn everything about her. Maybe it was the distraction of physical lust that drew him, or the challenge her evasions represented. Either would explain his growing obsession but not the desire to know her every secret. Whatever label stuck, he would only have to deal with it for a short time before she returned home.

One couple joined them at the telescopes, putting the eyes to the ones on the end. Waiting until they were engrossed and talking to each other, Ben shifted sideways, blocking most of Amie from their sight before sliding one hand up to tease her nipple. Even through her top and bra, the sensitive nub responded to his touch, hardening into a stiff point.

"Ben," she whispered, arching into his hand as

she looked toward the couple.

"Don't worry, I know what I'm doing and how far I can go." Before the temptation to push the boundaries grabbed hold, he stepped away, saying in the same quiet undertone, "I can't make it to the club tonight, but have lunch with me next Friday, and we'll go out to Spurs that night together."

She didn't hesitate, which pleased him. "I'm going to attend S.L. Anders' book signing at the library in the morning. Do you want me to meet you?"

"I'll pick you up at the library around noon. We have to start the ride back down in a few minutes, if you want to take any pictures."

Turning his attention to his other guests, he found himself looking forward to next weekend with an enthusiasm that had been lacking in his life for a while.

****

Amie started the car, watching Ben unsaddle the horses and wondering with a curl of jealousy what his plans were for tonight. As much as she would have liked to end last night and this evening giving in to her fantasy of a vacation fling, she wasn't sure she could go that far in a public club. Then again, she mused, pulling out of the parking space, before meeting Ben, she'd never imagined allowing someone to spank her, let alone in front of others. And from the way her sore backside last night sent arousal-spiking signals straight up her pussy every time she rolled over in bed, she didn't have to guess what her response might be to more of his control. Her nipple still tingled from his light touch, and she admitted the nearness of the other couple had added an extra spark, but that titillating moment was a far cry from baring herself in a room full of people.

The scene last night and the fun she'd had spending this afternoon listening to his deep voice filtering back to them along the rugged trail had given her a lot to think about, the least of which was her disappointment in not seeing Cal at Spurs. She would need to think about her plan and options going forward in her quest to seek justice for Myla while trying to decide how far she wanted to take things with Ben. She would love to toss aside her initial reason for this trip, get hot and naked, down and dirty with Ben instead, but her conscience and love for her friend wouldn't allow for that alone.

By the time she was climbing the stairs to her room at the B&B, she was too exhausted to drive out to Spurs. If she were honest with herself, she would admit returning to the club knowing Ben wouldn't be there held little appeal. Regardless of the delay in connecting with Cal, she spent a few hours reading before falling into bed to dream of a man who could turn her knees to jelly with one searing, green-eyed look.

A line had formed inside the library by the time Amie arrived on Friday morning at eleven. Other than one call from Ben last night confirming their lunch date, she hadn't heard from him since last weekend. That hadn't prevented her from reliving every word, every touch at the club and on the trail ride. She really needed to get him out of her system before returning home.

As a connoisseur of mystery and suspense novels, Ms. Anders topped her list of favorite authors. The book signing today surprised her, though, since this author had always kept her identity a secret, never putting her picture on her social media websites or book covers.

Amie went inside, but before she could get in line, she saw Lisa waving her over to a table. Relieved at seeing someone she knew, Amie didn't hesitate to accept her invitation to join her and the slender redhead sitting with her. Despite the crowd, people spoke in respectful low voices, a number of them browsing the bookshelves instead of spending time waiting in the long line.

"I've been watching for you. Come, sit with us." Lisa said, nudging the empty chair next to her. "Ben mentioned you were coming here. This is Poppy Flynn."

It shouldn't please her so much to hear Ben had spoken about her since last weekend, but there was a lot about this trip since meeting him that she hadn't anticipated. "Hi, Poppy." Amie sat down and glanced over at the attractive, dark-haired woman signing books. "So that's S.L. Anders."

"We know her as Skye. After her face and identity as an author was splashed across the Boise paper following the arrest of her husband's murderer, she decided she may as well come all the way out of the closet," Poppy said. "We're here for moral support."

"I hadn't heard that. I can't imagine how awful that would be." Her heart went out to the other woman.

"Oh, it gets worse." Lisa's voice revealed anger toward the individuals involved in causing her friend grief as she said, "When the truth came out, she learned someone she thought was a friend had set her up for a sham marriage so they could take half her inheritance in a divorce."

The calculating cruelty of some people never failed to surprise and sadden Amie. "Just when you think you've heard it all." The urge to confide her own drama with such scum nudged at her, but she didn't know Lisa, or Ben for that matter, well enough to trust them.

A tall, lean man with light, sandy hair and a rugged, tanned face stepped up behind the author and placed his hands on her shoulders, the move both supportive and proprietary. "Wow, the men around here are so hot."

Poppy laughed. "And you haven't met my Dakota. We were unable to make it last weekend until after you left. That's Clayton, Skye's new significant other and Dom."

Amie's gaze shot to the other woman, startled at the mention of the private club by someone else. How many in this small town knew about Spurs or were members?

"Oops. Did I catch you off guard? My bad." Poppy didn't appear sorry with her blue eyes twinkling and an impish grin curling the corners of her mouth. But her teasing put Amie at ease, and she returned her smile.

"I'm still getting used to what I let Ben do on

my first night," she admitted, glad to have someone who might understand what she was going through.

Lisa reached across the table and patted her hand. "It takes time to gather your wits around the new experiences and your reactions. Once you do, and accept them as normal needs for you, you'll love the rewards from the lifestyle and the right Dom. I've enjoyed submission for well over a year, but it wasn't until I came here and hooked up with Shawn that I was truly happy with my decision."

"Skye and I are almost as green as you, but once I set my sights on Dakota, there was no going back." Poppy nodded toward Skye. "There's a break in the lengthy line. You better take advantage of it. If you want to stick around, we're all going to lunch when she's done."

"Thank you so much," Amie said, warmed by the invitation. "But Ben has already invited me and will be here soon. Maybe another time? I'll be here for a few more weeks." She didn't know when she'd opted to stick with her original plan to stay a month, but she was more than happy with the decision.

"We'll set up something and get hold of you at Jen's place," Lisa offered.

"Thanks."

She turned and started toward the book-strewn table just as Ben walked in, his laser-sharp gaze zeroing in on her. Her heart executed the same slow roll as every other time, her body turning warm under his intense regard and the slow smile that creased his lean, rugged cheeks. She sucked in a much-needed breath as he came toward her, the compulsion to jump his bones right now, right here both titillating and shocking.

Well crap, do I have it bad, or what?

For now, she'd stick with the *or what*.

"Hey there." He eyed her tan slacks, brown pumps, and chocolate, soft cotton-stretchy pullover with approval before clasping her hand. "You look nice. Are you just getting in line to see Skye?"

"Yes, it's been too long up until now. Sorry."

"No need to apologize. I'm in no hurry. I'll visit with Clayton while you meet her."

As she got behind the only person left, he squeezed her hand then walked over to his friend who had joined Lisa and Poppy. She didn't realize she was staring after him so long until Skye cleared her throat, and Amie whipped her head around to see the author waiting for her with an amused glint in her dark eyes.

"Oh, sorry. I didn't mean to keep you waiting."

Skye gave an airy wave and chuckled. "Oh, trust

me, I understand. Been there, done that. In fact, I sometimes still have to kick myself to stay focused. My writing has suffered since meeting my guy." She extended a hand across the table. "Skye Anderson and also S.L. Anders. And you're Amie."

Amie shook her hand. "I can't get used to the small-town grapevine. Nice to meet you, and I know you must be tired of hearing it this morning, but I love your books." She picked up a copy of her latest and handed it over. "Do I pay you here?"

Skye opened the book and started writing. "I never tire of hearing it, so thank you, and consider it a welcome gift."

"Oh, but I'm just vacationing. I'm not moving here," she told her, touched by the offer.

"Funny, that's what I said, and so did Lisa and Poppy." Closing the book, she handed it back. "Clayton looked at me much the same as Ben eyed you when he came in. But, seriously, it will make me happy if you'll accept it as a gift. Just don't spread it around."

"Thank you, and I won't. It was nice to meet you."

"I'm sure we'll see each other again if you're going to continue seeing Ben while you're here."

Was she? She felt the heat of his large body

behind her before she realized he'd returned, her reaction as swift and consuming as every other time. Yes, she definitely was.

"If you're done here, I'm hungry."

So was she, but Amie didn't think it was food her body was craving. "I'm ready. Thanks, Skye. It was nice meeting you."

Ben led her outside to her car and opened the door. "I'll follow you back to the B&B then you can ride with me."

"Where are we going?" she asked, sliding behind the wheel, already missing his warm clasp. Soon she would need to examine why his simplest touch, his every look, and even his gestures heightened her senses more than the most intimate caresses from other men.

"My place. I've been working long hours lately and haven't spent as much time as I need to with my dogs. I've got chicken or brats to grill if either of those appeal to you."

A dog lover who wants to cook for me. No wonder all I can think about is sex when he's around.

"You choose. I like them both, and I'm not picky."

"Good enough."

****

Ben watched Amie closely for her reaction to his place as he pulled in front of the house. He liked the way her face had lit up when he'd mentioned his dogs and the spark of pleasure in those vivid, blue-green eyes when he'd told her they were having lunch at his place. He'd never been so intrigued by a woman's secrets before or looked forward to spending more time with someone with as much enthusiasm. The safety of tourists who were here, at least in part, for the outdoor activities their mountainous parks offered fell under his job description, and, given his suspicions she harbored a hidden agenda for this trip, it made sense he would want to keep a close eye on her.

Bart's death had driven home how easy and fast someone with a reckless streak, or, in her case, ulterior motives, could get themselves in trouble. He couldn't bear it if he wasn't there when someone else he cared about had needed him. Her secret would help determine why and how deeply his feelings for Amie would run. In the meantime, he had to keep reminding himself she was leaving in a few weeks, and to concentrate on helping her explore her interest in BDSM while making sure she didn't get into any more trouble like during her hike.

"This is nice out here." Before he could stop

her, she opened the door and hopped out, her gaze scanning his property with appreciation. She flipped him a wide smile over the hood. "I love the white fences, and are those llamas over there?" She pointed to the enclosed east pasture.

He nodded, coming around to open the front door. "Yeah, Mo and Larry. They were rescued from a hoarder a few years ago, and I adopted them after they were healthy enough to leave the shelter. I'll let the dogs out then, if you want, I'll introduce you."

"They're friendly?"

Shrugging, he waved her inside. "Sometimes. They're a work in progress as their earlier neglect left them with trust issues." He was about to warn her to stay behind him until he calmed the dogs, but she rushed forward and sank to her knees, laughing as they greeted her with tongue swipes.

"They're so cute!"

So was she. He should have suggested she wear jeans today but hadn't thought about it until now. Then again, she didn't seem to mind the dog hair. His cock twitched as he imagined his mouth and tongue all over her and her moans in his ear. Time to get a grip on himself and his pets.

Ben's shrill whistle got both the dogs and Amie's attention. "Treats then outside."

Pushing to her feet, she gave him an impish smile and reply that tested his control. "Am I included on getting a treat?"

He stepped toward her, and her eyes widened, the pulse in her neck jumping as he fisted his hands on his hips and leaned down to sink his teeth into the soft spot where her neck met her shoulder. Inhaling her scent went to his head, forcing him to release her soft skin and move back.

"*Their* treats are in the kitchen, under the sink. They'll love you for life if you give them one. Come on, I'll show you."

Her deep, indrawn breath lifted her breasts, drawing his gaze to the full mounds before he spun around and crossed the living area into the kitchen.

"I like how you kept the rustic charm of your house with the dark-wood beams and natural wood cabinets," she said, taking the bag of rawhide strips.

"Not a fan of the all-white kitchen craze?"

She wrinkled her nose, another trait he found cute. "Not so much. Too plain, boring."

Leaning against the counter, Ben crossed his arms and watched her. "Is that why you visited Spurs, out of boredom?" It wasn't nice to try to trip her up by asking her something she'd answered that night but a good way to catch a lie.

Amie avoided looking directly at him as she handed out the dog treats. "Curiosity, not boredom, as I said." She handed the bag back to him with a direct look. "Thanks. Do you have treats for the llamas?"

Score one for her. "Out in the barn." Grabbing her hand, he tugged her toward the back door, calling the dogs to follow. "They need a lot of fiber and like fresh vegetables and fruit for snacks. Mo and Larry are partial to sweet potatoes, and the horses prefer apples. If you drop one, the dogs will make off with it."

"Are they rescues also?"

"Along with the horses," he gestured toward the six grazing equines, "and the longhorn bull. That's Max." Stopping at the corral attached to the bull's stall, he smiled at her awed reaction to the large animal.

"*Wow*, that thing is huge."

"And dangerous if riled. Don't go near him," he warned.

"You don't have to tell me twice." Her stomach rumbled, and she blushed. "I skipped breakfast."

"You should have said something. I'll show you where the barrel of treats is in the barn, and you can go make nice with the horses and llamas while I start the grill. I'll be right over there." He pointed to the outdoor kitchen as they strode toward the barn. "I can see all the pastures from there."

"I'm happy to help."

"I've got it under control. If you don't want your clothes to get any dirtier, though, you might not want to trek out in the fields."

"They'll wash, and I may never get another chance to make nice with llamas."

Returning her grin, he gave her hair a quick yank before tugging her inside the barn. He was discovering more and more to like about Amie Buchanon, and the more he liked her, the more he wanted her.

Ben showed her the llama and horse stalls, her eyes going soft when he mentioned the two miniatures shared one space because they didn't like to be separated. "Do you have a pet?" he asked, leading the way to the tack room where he kept a barrel stocked with handouts.

"No. I live in an apartment, and it wouldn't be fair to a dog. Maybe someday though. I'm saving to buy a house." She reached for two yams. "They really like these?"

He nodded, remembering his doubt when he'd been told that. "They'll devour them in no time."

There was a lot he didn't know about her, starting with why she'd really traveled to Mountain Bend on her own for an extended stay and including how far she wished to take exploring his sexual lifestyle. To get where he wanted to go with her, he would start with the latter and work his way into getting her to spill the truth, hopefully without pissing her off or driving her away.

He'd never been above playing dirty and sneaky to get what he wanted. "Tell me," he stated, cupping her shoulders, "do you have any lingering effects or questions from your first night exploring submission?" Moving forward with slow, measured steps, he backed her up against the barrel-shaped wooden saddle stand and took the yams from her hands. Setting them aside, he braced his hands behind her on the smooth wood, relishing the hitch in her breathing.

"No, I'm fine."

"*Mmmm,* I didn't do a very good job then. Either that, or you're not being completely honest. Which is it?"

Amie frowned. "What do you mean?"

"You want me to spell it out? Okay." He reached behind her, squeezed her ass, and she bit her lower lip. "I can tell by your face you're remembering the soreness, which is what I expected and you should have answered. I did mention the importance of honesty."

"The small amount of soreness wasn't anything that lasted long, or I couldn't handle," she returned, her tone defiant and challenging.

Changing tactics, he slid one hand to her hip where he noticed the side zipper to her pants. "That may be true," he said, lowering the zipper, "but if you want to return to Spurs with me tonight, you'll need to do better when I ask you something." Her face reddened, but she remained silent and still as he slipped his hand inside her slacks, placed his palm between her legs and ran one finger under her panties to trace over her plump, damp labia. "Do you want to return with me?"

Sucking in a breath, she closed her eyes and arched against his hand, nodding. "*Yes.*"

Ben dipped between her folds and brushed his finger over her clit, watching as her breathing grew labored. "Enough to answer with honesty instead of giving me an evasive reply to even simple inquiries?"

"I will," she hurried to agree.

"Open your eyes, Amie," he instructed, circling the swollen bud. She was soft and wet, a temptation he was hard-pressed to hold back from, especially when she obeyed, and he saw the depth of her need reflected in her bright gaze.

"Any time I ask you something, I want the truth, no sidestepping." He pressed deeper inside her, and she gasped, her hands flying to his waist to anchor herself.

"Got it. Ben, *please.*"

Satisfied she would remember this conversation, he removed his hand, her face going from pink and aroused to red and frustrated by the time he zipped her pants. He returned the sweet potatoes to her hands, saying, "I have to get the grill started if we're going to eat. Don't wander off too far."

Pivoting, Ben walked out before she found her tongue.

Chapter Six

Amie glared at Ben's retreating back, her body still quivering with need, burning for his touch. She'd been enjoying his company, the tour of his property, his animals, and the fantasies running through her head. Then he'd gone and done *that*. What the heck was it about him that never failed to turn her inside out, and why did she continue to crave more even when he irritated her?

Yes, she still found it easy to recall the lingering achiness from his spanking last week, that pleasant reminder of her first experience and the surprising arousal from the heat and sting she'd reaped from his hard hand. But she'd seen no need to mention it and wasn't used to baring her innermost thoughts with anyone except Myla. Of course, the men who had come and gone in her life before Ben had never shown such interest in her either.

And she liked that about him, maybe too much

because she shuddered to think what his reaction would be to learning what had prompted her trip to this area.

Squaring her shoulders, she left the sweet hay-scented barn, figuring she wouldn't find answers standing around. As she watched where she was stepping crossing the field toward the llamas with two of the dogs bouncing along beside her, she wished she'd worn more comfortable clothes and shoes. She'd dressed for a date at a restaurant, not an afternoon on his spread, yet she couldn't imagine having more fun with him anywhere else except the club, even with her frustrated libido still clamoring for release.

"Well hello, guys," she crooned to the woolly animals as the pair trotted up to the fence.

Ben wasn't kidding when he said they loved sweet potatoes. She'd no sooner held them out to each one and they snatched them up. Laughing, she tentatively reached out to stroke the brown-and-white one, marveling at the soft, curly coat. It broke her heart to think they'd suffered before coming here. If she hadn't already been enamored of their owner, today would have sealed the deal.

Sighing, she wondered what she was going to do about her growing attraction and her quest to find Miller and at least attempt to get a revealing comment from him. She was no detective or actress, which made her question how she'd ever thought this plan was feasible. And here she'd believed she'd left her penchant for getting herself into untenable situations behind along with her childhood.

But even admitting the unlikelihood of success, Amie couldn't bring herself to give up on the idea yet. All that was necessary to harden her resolve was to remember the pain of losing Mike and seeing Myla's struggle to recover. Besides, it would give her an excuse to hang around and continue seeing Ben. Last week and just now, he'd piqued her interest in alternative sex, something she would have sworn before coming here wasn't her thing. She couldn't return to her boring life and stagnant sex with someone else without exploring with him further and determining whether it was him or the kink she craved most.

The llamas trotted off, and she took a moment to toss a stick the dogs dropped at her feet before starting toward the horses with the apple she'd managed to keep hold of while treating the llamas. Halfway toward the other fenced pasture, a rifle shot ricocheted from the surrounding forests, catching her off guard with how close it sounded. Ben's alarmed shout startled her seconds later, right before his arms locked around her waist and he tackled her to the ground. With a grunt, he landed first with her sprawled on top of him before twisting until she lay under the protective cover of his large body.

"Ben!" she gasped in alarm, her heartbeat slamming against her chest as a second rifle shot echoed from the woods high in the surrounding hills, this bullet hitting a nearby fence post.

"Stay still," he snapped, lifting his head to survey the direction the shots came from with an icy glare, his chest heaving against hers with his harsh breathing.

Other than the spooked horses' frightened whinnies, silence transpired the minutes following the loud reports. With his weight pressing her into the ground, Amie grew uncomfortable, but she kept quiet and still, waiting for his directive. She assumed the gunfire had been a careless hunter not paying attention, but how did Ben know in time to dash from the back of the house and warn her?

"I think we're good, but, to be sure, let's get to the house." Ben slowly got to his feet, keeping an eye on the surrounding hills as he held a hand down to Amie.

Holding tight, she kept up with him as he

hightailed it across the range and pulled her behind the first small stable. "Are you all right?" His voice and gaze reflected concern as he paused to run his hand down her back and lightly brush off her butt and thighs.

She pushed her hair aside with the back of her free hand, still clinging to his with the other. "Just a little shaky from the suddenness of the whole mishap."

Even that impersonal touch ignited a longing for more inside her she found difficult to ignore. Given the stressful circumstances, Amie figured she was sick, a sexual pervert, or there was something in all this fresh air responsible for her uncharacteristic and questionable responses to Ben.

I mean really, what else could it be? She still trembled from that startling, possibly harmful close call, yet all she could think about was getting naked with her hot rescuer.

"Mishap my ass. Pure no-excuse-acceptable carelessness. Let's return to the house. You can wash up while I bring the food in."

She managed to keep up with his brisk, long-legged stride, her nerves steadying once they reached the patio. "How did you know?" She'd never imagined hunters would wander close enough to the ranches for such accidents.

"The sun hit the rifle scope, causing a flash, and when it didn't shift in another direction before the first shot, I didn't take any chances, which turned out to be the right decision."

Even though the second bullet struck a post several yards from them, Amie would have been twice as scared had she been caught unaware alone. "Thanks for your quick thinking." The dogs were already by the door, and she bent to pet the smaller female, who shook and cowered. "It's okay, baby."

Ben opened the door then turned off the gas grill. "Thanks for not panicking. Bathroom is down the hall, first door on the left. I'll see to the dogs," he added when she cast a worried look toward them.

"Okay. I'll only be a few minutes."

Ben drew his first steady breath when Amie entered the house, his muscles still in knots from that scare. When he'd seen the glint from a rifle scope up in the hills, he hadn't thought much of it until it remained steady toward the direction of his ranch. His mouth had gone dry from the possibilities running through his head and, unwilling to take any chances with either his guest or his animals, he'd sprinted toward them. It wasn't until the first shot rang out that heart-pounding terror had spurred him into getting to Amie faster.

Not since the last time he'd rushed to Bart's rescue had he experience such gut-cramping fear for someone, his first immediate thought he couldn't arrive too late again. He hadn't been late to rescue Bart from the rodeo accident, but away from him amounted to the same thing when panic grabbed him by the balls. God, it made no fucking sense for him to overreact, or for such dread to grip him and rob him of common sense when he thought of Amie getting hurt. But his emotions since meeting her were unlike anything he'd felt toward another woman and required closer examination soon.

Stacking the sausages and corn on the cob on a serving plate, he went inside, checked the dogs then gave them another treat. He'd just finished setting the kitchen table when she emerged from the bathroom appearing refreshed and calm, a hungry look on her face that he could attribute to either the food or him since her gaze bounced between both.

Too bad now was not the time to pick up where they'd left off in the barn. Ben couldn't take advantage of any vulnerability she might experience from that scare, and giving in to his own need raging from the incident was not wise. As she crossed through the living area, he caught her subtle glances at the furniture and around the room, as if she were searching for something. He recalled her doing the same thing when they'd first arrived.

Curious, he asked, "Looking for something in particular?"

He could see the wheels turning in her head as she moved to the table contemplating what to say. She pleased him with an honest reply and her inquisitiveness. "I was wondering if you have restraints here, or if you limit your kink preferences to the club."

Waving to the chair for her to sit, he placed a brat and corn on her plate, saying, "No restraints, but I do have a few props and toys in my closet."

Picking up her fork, she nodded at her plate. "Thanks. Why not?"

"Two reasons," he said, sitting down. "One, I've never invited a woman here with the intention of doing a scene, and, two, if I ever did, it would allow me to get creative." Her eyes lit up at that, and he doubted she realized her interest in submission probably wasn't a fleeting whim.

"Like how?" Taking a bite of the sausage, she kept her curious gaze on him.

"Well, I could use a belt or tie instead of cuffs and

straps, attach them to the sofa or chair legs, maybe bind your hands behind you and bend you over this table." She took a bite, and he watched her throat work from the picture he'd planted in her head. "If I'm in a sadistic mood, I might stand you in front of the windows on a cold day, tell you to bend over, then tie your wrists to your ankles. But don't worry, I wouldn't let you topple over. *Ahhh,*" he sighed with fake dramatic emphasis, "the possibilities are endless. And those are in the house. The barns and outdoors open up all kinds of prospects."

Amie frowned with censure. "You were sadistic when you left me in the barn earlier."

"No, I was making a point. There's a difference."

"If you say so."

Unable to resist, he insisted in a hard, gruff voice, "Go to the club with me tonight, and I'll make it up to you."

Amie answered with a slow smile and no hesitation. "Okay."

****

Cal Miller was still laughing as he crept away from his perch that had offered a perfect view and aim at the small ranch in the valley below. He'd damn near fallen when he'd recognized Amie Buchanon, that pesky Norton chick's best friend. No way her presence in the area was a coincidence, just like he'd known Mike's sister hadn't happened to be visiting the same private club he belonged to, the one where he'd first met her brother.

Did they think he was stupid? Not only had Mike talked incessantly about his sister and her best friend, but he'd kept a picture of the girls on his refrigerator. Twelve years might have passed since he'd seen that photo, but neither had changed that much. He hadn't gotten away with his fun and games for years by not paying attention to his surroundings and the people he'd either pissed off or upset. That was one reason why he traveled a lot, applied for temporary guest passes at clubs, hunted around the country and some overseas. By the time he returned to scenes of his crimes, enough time had usually passed that no one would remember him, or he'd kept to himself enough no one had seen him.

In all these years, the only mistake he'd made had been with Mike. He never should have hooked up with someone so young and naïve. He'd let the kid's adoration go to his head and, when he'd tired of him, Mike hadn't taken it well. It wasn't Cal's fault his blunt, calloused words had sent him over that railing. Then again, he hadn't tried stopping him either. Standing right next to him, and being much larger, he could have easily prevented his death. He recalled the kick and rush he'd experienced watching his young lover plummet to the ground, his scream drawing his smile.

Cal trekked through the woods wishing he'd fired upon one of the animals. Not only was he craving the sight of blood, but he would have found the couple's horrified reaction amusing. Yeah, he was a sadistic bastard, but it wasn't his fault he bored easily. Discovering the Buchanon girl's presence had livened things up, and he could already think of fun things to do to her for extra entertainment. He wondered if she was as stupid as her friend and would join a club in the hopes of finding him and something on him.

Talk about icing on the cake for added fun. And maybe, afterward, he wouldn't stop at running her off the road. There were any number of secluded, empty cabins in the mountains he could break into, and, if he could lure her to one, the possibilities were endless.

One could only hope.

****

All Amie could think about as Ben drove her

back to the B&B was the relief he promised her that night. She wanted him with every cell in her body, and even looked forward to trying something new with bondage, but she was on the fence about how far to go in public or trying a spanking implement other than his hand. The snap of his calloused flesh striking hers had added an intimacy to the episode, even over her skirt and then panties, which had heightened her arousal. Without any other experiences to judge by, she assumed that was normal, at least for her.

When he pulled in front of Miner's Junction, his phone buzzed, after checking the caller identification, he held up a hand for her to wait. "Hold on, I have to get this," he said before answering. "Hey, Kevin, what's up?"

Ben's expression hardened as he listened, and Amie guessed the news wasn't good. "Yeah, sure. Give me about thirty to forty minutes to get there." He hung up. "Fuck."

She reached over and laid a hand on his rigid forearm. "What's wrong?"

"I have to meet the deputy sheriff where some campers found a dead bear, so I'll have to see you at Spurs later. I'll ask Drew if you can ride out with them."

"That's fine, but what aren't you saying?

There's more to the animal's death, isn't there?" She could tell by the fury swirling in his eyes and his taut jaw that something else had occurred regarding the bear.

Shaking his head, he squeezed her hand. "It wasn't a quick or painless death, and that's all I'm saying." Wrapping his hand around her wrist, he pulled her over, holding her arm between them as he ravaged her mouth.

Like every other time he touched her, Amie went hot and succumbed to his control without thought or hesitation. With a groan, she melted against him, a surge of heat going through her when she tried to slide her arm out from between them to wrap around his broad shoulders. *It's from the extra adrenaline caused by the afternoon's events. That has to be it, right*?

That was her excuse, and, as he released her and her lips throbbed in tune with her rapid heartbeat, she decided she was sticking with that explanation. Otherwise, it would mean she was in jeopardy of getting into this relationship deep enough to sink, and she never was a good swimmer.

"I'll get to the club as soon as I can. Try not to get into any mischief."

"Hey, today wasn't my fault, and I didn't mean

to hold up the hiking group that time."

"Still," he drawled, "trouble seems to follow you." She opened her mouth to apologize, but he laid a finger over her lips. "Go before you piss me off."

"Well, I wouldn't want to do that." At least, not before he relieved the sexual tension he'd proven so good at building inside her. "Thank you for lunch. I'll see you tonight."

Jen stood behind the guest counter when Amie entered, and she remembered Drew's presence at Spurs when Ben had her over the bench. The few times she'd seen Jen this past week, the proprietress had been too busy to do anything except ask in passing if she needed anything. Amie couldn't prevent the warm flush spreading over her face, but Jen let her know there was nothing to feel uncomfortable about when she smiled and welcomed her.

"There you are. I was hoping to catch you this evening." As soon as Amie reached her, she asserted in a quiet undertone, "I'm so glad you gave Spurs a try. How'd you like having Ben to yourself all night?"

"He was very...helpful," she replied, unable to come up with another adjective at the moment. "Have you and Drew been members for long?"

"Oh yeah. Submitting is a great stress-reliever. All you have to do is put yourself into a trustworthy

Dom's hands and let him take over for a few hours, most of the time ending the night relaxed and feeling really good if you haven't earned a Dom's displeasure for an infraction. We're good friends with Randy Daniels, the original owner. He sold it before moving, but we keep in touch. He opened it about seven, eight years ago. Are you interested enough to go again?"

Amie relaxed, pleased Jen was making this easy for her and was so open about her involvement. "Yes. Ben invited me but then got called into work and will meet me there." She meant to stop there, but curiosity got the better of her, and she asked, "Does that happen often, doing something wrong that lands you trouble?"

"It depends. Kathie loves goading the Masters, and most of the consequences. Me, I like it all, the lighter stuff and, on occasion, a harsher scene. A lot depends on my mood, and Drew's. It takes a while to learn what works for you, so, if that was your first visit to a club, take your time exploring. You don't want to rush into something out of curiosity only to discover it's a big turn-off for you. Come on down in about an hour and ride out with us."

"Thanks, I'll do that. Ben was going to ask Drew for the favor," she said, grateful for the open dialogue. "Got any suggestions on what I should wear?"

"I'd offer you something from my fetish stash, but there's no way your boobs will fit in anything I have. Do you have any camisoles or boy shorts sleepwear? Those would work," she suggested.

Picturing her nightwear and undergarments, Amie nodded. "I do. Good idea, thanks. See you soon."

An hour later, Amie stood in indecision in front of the bathroom mirror. The teal silk camisole-and-boy-shorts set she had only worn to bed showcased her full figure without being revealing. But that didn't keep the thin material from clinging to every bump of her areola and her nipples, or her breasts from shifting as she moved without a bra. The shorts didn't allow for panty lines, and she found the slide of silk against her bare bottom and labia both titillating and distracting. She enjoyed the pleasant, arousing sensations, but that was here, alone in her room, not in front of a large gathering of people she barely knew.

Except Ben. Even though they'd met less than two weeks ago, the incident that had brought them together when she'd slipped away from the hiking group and the disruption on his ranch that afternoon were harrowing enough she'd let her guard down and had drawn closer to him than she had any other man. It couldn't lead to anything, not with her returning to Omaha soon. That reminder alone should douse her feelings and keep her head on straight when they were together.

Should, but hadn't as of yet.

Checking the time, she swore, realizing she couldn't stall any longer. Either she wore this or the same skirt as last time. She pictured Ben's face when he saw her in the lingerie outfit and donned her jeans over the shorts and a sweatshirt to cover the camisole until they got to the club.

What the heck, she decided, skipping downstairs. Like she reminded herself, she would return home soon and never see any of these people again, so no biggie, right? And the tight clutch in her chest accompanying that thought was just heartburn, nothing else.

Jen was waiting for Amie while Drew pulled the car around. "Sorry. I hope I haven't kept you."

"Not at all. I just finished giving Tanya instructions. Our two couples are out for the evening, and with you gone, she doesn't have much to do. You're right on time." Jen started for the front door, asking over her shoulder, "Did you find something to wear?"

"Yes. I'll change out of my jeans when we get there. I'm not used to going out in bare legs when it's this cool."

Jen laughed as they walked out to the car. "Then, don't stick around too long. Winters here are butt-numbing cold."

"They can be at home, too, but usually not too early, or for too long."

Funny how the mention of longer, colder winters didn't sound as off-putting as Amie would have thought given her dislike of frigid temperatures. Maybe because all she needed for warmth was to think about being with Ben. The best thing she could do at this point was get as much out of this trip and her first vacation fling as she could and return home with fond memories to share with Myla, since the odds of her original reason for coming here panning out were slim.

Like the few men who had come before him, he was sure to do something to upset her or turn her off or anger her, and that would be that.

Lisa, Poppy, and Skye, sitting in a lounge area with several other girls, waved to them. Maybe it was their immediate welcome, or that she didn't stand out like a newcomer tonight wearing the lingerie set, but as she and Jen wound their way over, Amie didn't feel as uncomfortable as last time. She returned greetings and flushed under appreciative gazes, tonight from pleasure rather than embarrassment. She guessed it was her decision to reap as many rewards as she could from her short stay here that was making this easier.

Now, if only Ben would arrive soon. Like any woman, she enjoyed attention from men, but her body only pulsed for his touch, and it was only him occupying her thoughts even when he wasn't around.

"I'm glad you made it back tonight, Amie," Lisa said as Amie took a chair across from the small sofa where Lisa sat next to Skye. "The guys are finalizing some details about a fundraiser game night they're planning. Will you still be here in two weeks? It should be fun."

Jen answered with a teasing grin before Amie could give a noncommittal reply. "She booked her room for a month, so let's hold her to it."

"Careful, Amie. These guys can charm the pants off you, literally, and then turn around and torture you in the most devious, frustrating ways," Poppy warned. "Who knows what they're planning behind those closed doors."

"Says the girl who went after the baddest Dom

here without batting an eye," Jen drawled.

Poppy flashed a quick grin. "What can I say? Between the attitude and the body, I was a goner at first sight. Bet it was the same for you with Ben, Amie."

"You've snagged our Ben? Damn, when are you leaving?"

"Kathie!" Several of them exclaimed together.

Amie couldn't take offense at the younger girl. Her mischievous grin proved she wasn't serious. "Don't worry. You can have him back after I leave." Now why did saying that cause her chest to constrict again? That must stop.

To take her mind off her unwise growing feelings for Ben, she scanned the room while listening to the girls chatter. It was obvious they were close, and their bond made her miss Myla even though they talked every day. There weren't as many scenes taking place with several of the Doms holed up in a meeting, but two couples were on the dance floor and one at a chain station. The rest mingled around the tables and bar, and that's where she spotted Cal Miller then went cold with shock.

She'd been so immersed with thoughts of Ben and what he would do tonight, she hadn't considered Cal might make an appearance. It was what she'd banked on when coming here, what she'd hoped for, yet her hands turned clammy just thinking about approaching him. Other than older with more gray in his hair, he didn't look much different from the picture Myla gave her of him and Mike. Lucky for her, they'd never met.

If she were going to strike up a conversation with him, now was the time, before Ben arrived and before she chickened out altogether. Taking a deep breath, she stood. "Excuse me. I think I'll get something to drink. Be right back."

As Amie approached the bar, she became conscious of her skimpy attire and uneasy about getting close to Miller, especially while wearing next to nothing. Then she remembered his sexual preference and relaxed. He might look but wouldn't be interested, which helped boost her bravado.

She didn't realize what a big man Cal was until she slid onto the stool next to him, unprepared for the nerve-racking sly calculation in his dark eyes when he glanced down at her. At least he made it easy by starting a conversation.

"Hi, there. Master Miller." He held out a beefy hand, which she gave a quick clasp before pulling back.

"Nice to meet you, Sir. I'm...Amelia." Amie

opted for her full name just in case Mike had mentioned his sister's friend.

"Amelia, that's a pretty name for a pretty girl. Have you been a member here long?" He sipped his beer, but those cold eyes never left her face.

"No, I'm still new to all this and waiting for Master Ben, who's guiding me along." She hadn't planned on bringing up Ben, but something about the way Cal's beady eyes kept assessing her put her on guard.

Needing something for her dry throat, she signaled the bartender, someone she hadn't met yet, and asked for a rum and Coke.

"I'll take another," Cal said, holding up his empty bottle.

"Sorry, that was your second. I can get you something else."

"That's a fucking stupid rule. Another beer won't impair my judgment. I'm not a kid," Cal snapped.

Amie didn't know the Dom's name, but she wouldn't want him looking her way with the icy glare he leveled at Cal. "You're welcome to leave, Miller. I'll get you your drink, Amie."

Somehow, she wasn't surprised he knew her name. With the exception of the jerk next to her, all the men here seemed to possess a protective attitude toward the members and the club's reputation.

"What do you say we split this place, go somewhere else for a drink together. I'd like to get to know you better, Amelia."

No way in hell. She didn't want to piss him off, so she used Ben as an excuse. "Thanks, but I already promised Master Ben I'd wait for him."

"Well, maybe another time. I'll be in the area for another few weeks before heading back to Omaha."

She jumped at the opening, surprised it came from him without her prodding. "What a coincidence. It's a small world. I'm visiting here from Omaha, too. Born and raised there. How about you?"

Cal rubbed his jaw, a small smile she didn't trust playing around his lips. "Same. Too bad we didn't meet before."

"Yes, well, it's a big city, and I don't go out much." The bartender returned with her drink, and she nodded her thanks.

"You need anything else, let me know." He spoke to her, but his eyes included Cal.

"Thank you, I will."

"Pansy," Cal sneered before giving her a bland look. "What brings you here if you don't go out at home? Think word won't get back to your friends about your interest in kink, or maybe a friend talked you into giving it a try?"

The hairs on the back of her neck rose in suspicion. That guess was hitting too close to the truth. Coming up with answers was harder than she imagined.

"No, just satisfying my curiosity, and some people recommended Spurs." Amie picked up her glass, more than ready to get away from him when his gaze kept sliding down to her breasts. "It was nice talking with you."

Lightning fast, he grabbed her arm, his bruising grip startling her into dropping the glass. "Not so fast, sub. I'm ready to play, and your Dom isn't here yet..."

"Wrong. Let her go. Now."

Chapter Seven

It took every ounce of Ben's control not to slam his fist into the bastard's smug face as he released Amie's arm. Neither had seen him approaching, and he'd stepped up behind them the same time Nick was also coming to intervene from behind the bar. Seeing any man grab a woman like that would piss him off, but Amie's pale face and spasm of alarm had sent his rage skyrocketing.

Withdrawing his hand, the man leaned back, his expression going from arrogant to contrite. "Sorry. It was a misunderstanding is all."

"I'll bet," Nick muttered.

Ben looked at Amie and saw the anger in her eyes, glad she hadn't let him upset her. Which didn't explain her answer when he asked, "Is that right, Amie?"

"More a lack of communication." Turning to the other man, she said, "As you can see, Master Ben has arrived, so if you'll excuse me?"

She reached for his hand, a first for her, and her cold, shaky fingers gave her away. Her bravado was as false as her explanation. Either she didn't want to make a scene, or there was more between the two than either was saying.

"Of course. Nice meeting you, Amelia," Cal drawled, his tone laced with sarcasm.

"You might brush up on the rules if you plan to return, Miller," Nick advised. "Your membership is temporary."

Miller nodded, his eyes ice-cold as he stalked off. Ben thought his camouflage hunting attire odd for the club scene, but that wasn't as questionable as his behavior and attitude, especially for a guest.

Drawing Amie closer, he told Nick, "We need to keep an eye on him."

"Please, Ben, not because of me. I'm sorry. I don't want to cause problems for anyone. Maybe he had a bad day."

"That doesn't give him the right to do this, *Amelia*." He held up her arm where bruises were already forming and saw her blanch. He'd ask her about giving Miller her full name later.

The owners of the club and Drew joined them just then, Shawn's rigid expression boding ill for

Miller as he demanded, "What's going on here?"

Dakota growled and Clayton crossed his arms and wore his prosecutor's face.

Ben didn't care for Amie being the center of attention any more than she did from the discomfort she portrayed by fidgeting and bracing her free arm across her waist. He just noticed her lingerie and appreciated how the silk clung to her round breasts and pert nipples and the shorts hugged her hips. But he could see she wasn't used to standing in front of five disgruntled Doms in such skimpy attire, which was adding to her embarrassment.

"Miller got out of line," Nick said.

"I told you I didn't like him," Dakota growled.

Clayton sighed and rolled his eyes. "Dakota, you don't like anyone."

"And now you know why."

Shawn held up a hand. "Are you all right, little one?" he asked Amie in a softer tone.

"Yes, thank you. It really was an unfortunate misunderstanding, and I'd rather you let it go."

Ben didn't understand her evasive dismissal when he could see her exchange with Miller bothered her, but it wasn't the first time her behavior hinted at something else going on with her. "That's their call."

"He looks familiar," Drew put in, glancing

toward Miller who appeared to be negotiating a scene with Linda, a regular member. "He stayed a night at our place not long ago, just until the cabin he rented was cleaned. He seemed friendly enough then."

"I'm up first for monitoring, and I'll make sure I keep an eye on him." Clayton watched Miller lead Linda to the new bondage chair then strolled that way.

"Amie, please go sit with the girls while I talk to Shawn about the meeting I missed." Ben placed his hand on her lower back and nudged her toward the group watching from the seating area.

"Sure."

He waited until she was out of earshot before saying, "Sorry I'm late. We found another carcass with signs of deliberate maiming."

Dakota swore. "Assholes are out in full force lately. I can go tracking tomorrow."

Dakota was the best tracker around, but they were still looking for a needle in a haystack when Ben thought of how many hunters were in the area and the land available for them to cover.

"I appreciate it, but until I get something or someone to focus on, we may as well save our time. The park staff has been asked to spread the word to tourists. With luck, if he catches wind people are on alert, he'll back off, maybe leave."

"That doesn't stop him though."

As sheriff, Shawn would rather see the bastard in jail, as would Ben, but Ben would settle for a fast end to the tortuous deaths if that's the best they could do.

Leaning against the bar, he took the beer Nick handed him with thanks before telling Shawn, "If you've got a way to do that, I'm all ears. In the meantime, where are we at with McCullough's fundraiser?"

"Two weeks from tonight. I spoke with Gavin, and he cleared the date with Cody and Olivia. Drake can make it that weekend also. We'll have to hustle, but we have to take advantage of the decent weather and when the three of them can get away together."

"When's the next planning session?" Drew asked. "Or did I miss that earlier?"

"We decided on meeting at the ranch next Sunday to finalize the games, prizes, and cost." Shawn flicked Dakota a mocking grin. "With some arm twisting."

Dakota grunted. "Too much fucking socializing. Poppy needs to rest."

When they all laughed at that bald-faced

exaggeration, even Dakota's lips twitched. "Okay, maybe I'm using her as an excuse. Don't tell her. I'll never hear the end of it."

"I've always said a good woman can change a man," Drew quipped. "Speaking of which, it looks like ours are tired of waiting on us."

Ben turned and saw Amie following Lisa, Poppy, Skye, and Jen out back. He wondered if she would brave stripping and joining them in the hot tub or would choose to keep warm in one of the robes they provided. When they'd moved the bar from the center of the room along the side, it opened up the space to give a clear, straight view all the way to the back glass doors, but with people constantly moving about, he couldn't keep a close eye on her face. He doubted if she realized it, but her striking blue-green eyes and facial expressions gave away more than any of her words.

"Excuse me," he said. "I'll see if Clayton needs a hand."

"Yeah, right." Dakota snorted. "And everyone says I'm whipped."

"You are," Ben tossed over his shoulder. "I'm just doing my job as Amie's assigned Dom." He didn't believe that any more than his friends.

****

"I'll wait here," Amie said when they reached the glass sliders that opened onto the rear deck and hot tub. She wanted to be sure she would go through with undressing and joining them before going out and then balking at the last minute.

"If you don't want to get in, grab a robe from that closet and sit on the edge. They're plenty warm enough." Poppy showed her where the robes were stashed.

Not wanting to stand out, she liked that idea better than waiting in indecision on the inside. "I'll do that. Thanks."

Jen held the door open. "Hey, we were all newbies once, and Skye here isn't much more experienced than you."

"That's right. It's nice to have someone take my place as the kink virgin."

Following her outside, Amie chuckled at her label. "What do I have to do to shed the title?"

"Get more experience." Lisa eyed her askance as she slipped off her sheath. "Which, from the way Ben jumped to your defense and has been eyeing you since, I have to ask, what are you waiting for?" She dropped her panties and wasted no time sinking into the hot, bubbly water with an appreciative sigh.

Good question. And one Amie hoped to answer

tonight. She'd wanted Ben before he'd arrived in time to come to her defense in a way no man had before, and now all she needed to decide was when, where, and how. Or let him choose. Yes, that sounded much better. She didn't want the stress of making decisions and wondering if they were right, what he wanted, or how she compared to those with more knowledge on what worked for them.

Amie bundled in a white, fluffy robe, hiked it up to her knees, and perched on the tub's ledge with her feet resting on the seat underwater, yet still felt like the outsider with the four of them enjoying the tub without an ounce of self-consciousness. She could picture Myla fitting in here with them, teasing her while she soaked in the bubbly heated water, and she was struck with a wave of homesickness.

"Hey, I'm sorry," Lisa said, laying a wet hand on her arm. "It's none of my business. I didn't mean to pry."

"You didn't. I was thinking about my best friend. She's going through a rough time right now trying to overcome a physical trauma, and I miss her. To answer your question, I'm hoping he'll take me further tonight."

"Been there, done that. Maybe your friend needs to hook up with a good Dom when she's up to it," Poppy suggested before sinking down to her shoulders, the water turning the ends of her bright red hair darker.

"She's got a nice guy who's crazy about her, if she doesn't let her attitude drive him away." The last time they spoke, Myla had seemed more open toward Matt, but that could change once she was released from rehab, and if she returned to seeking revenge for Mike's death.

After meeting Cal Miller face-to-face, there was no way she wanted Myla going after him any more than she wanted another confrontation.

"If you wish to pursue things with your guy, I suggest you join us. They can't resist wet, slick skin." Jen splashed Amie's legs, grinning.

"I hadn't considered that. Good point."

It wasn't getting naked in front of the girls that bothered her but the crowd inside. And not even her shyness about such public exposure was much of a deterrent considering how much she wanted Ben tonight, but the thought of Cal Miller's cold eyes on her naked flesh creeped her out. She couldn't see him from where she sat, which helped when she stood and dropped the robe before she could talk herself out of it.

The cold night air stung her bare skin, and she

quickly stripped off the lingerie and slid into the steaming water, settling next to Jen. "Oh God, this feels wonderful." Sighing, she sank down until the heat bubbled around her shoulders.

Talk turned to the club's upcoming fundraiser and the game night planned to raise money for a women's shelter. It sounded like fun, but since her original plan to get Cal to reveal something incriminating changed the moment she met the guy and realized the risk and futility of her idea, there was no reason for her to stick around that long.

Except for one. Ben.

How had she become so needy for the man in such a brief time? Was it the chance to take a walk on the wild, forbidden side without anyone back home knowing and her recent sexual dry spell that accounted for her obsession, or the possibility something deeper and meaningful could develop? If she were honest with herself, she'd admit she would be open to the latter if they didn't live so far apart.

Jen nudged her, getting her attention. "Heads-up, Amie. Incoming hot guys, and only one is mine."

Her eyes flew open as Drew and Ben came out, Ben's serious expression never changing as he strode up behind her and lifted her from the tub. Bending, he grabbed the robe and bundled her up, the soft, thick terry cloth as warm as his body.

"Ladies, if you'll excuse us." Picking up her camisole and shorts, he handed them to her and ushered her inside.

Bemused and excited by his take-charge attitude, Amie noticed Drew tugging Jen out as she lifted a hand to them, not sure what to say.

"Have fun, Amie," Poppy called out, her voice laced with amusement.

"Talk first, then we'll see about fun," Ben said, his rigid tone drawing her gaze up to his tense face.

"About?" Clutching her clothes, she avoided looking at anyone else as he led her to a small, three-sided alcove carved out around the stacks of hay bales along one wall, only big enough for the one wide armchair. The half walls offered some privacy, but anyone close enough could see over or glance at them from the one open side.

Settling in the chair, he tugged her onto his lap and plucked the undergarments from her hand to set them up on the hay ledge. With one arm banded around her waist, he slid his free hand inside the robe to rest his warm, rough palm on her upper thigh, her only thought how close he was to her aching flesh.

"For starters, tell me if you left anything out of your exchange with Miller. I didn't care for you making excuses for him."

Amie thought of telling him everything, but what would be the point since she'd ditched her original idea? If she wanted to reap as much from her time with him as possible, she'd rather not waste it arguing, or possibly turning him away from her by revealing she'd omitted the real reason for her trip. He was kind of a stickler for full honesty.

"No, I didn't. He seemed nice until he grabbed for me, and I didn't lead him on, if that's what you're thinking." That hadn't occurred to her until just now, and she looked up at him to see his reaction.

He lifted a brow as he rubbed her thigh. "It's not. You're not exactly open and forthcoming about a lot of things, but you're also not a tease. Are you keeping anything from me I need to know, Amie?"

"No, not that I can think of." *Not anymore.* "But if you mean in regards to what you need from me here, remember, I'm still feeling my way through with all of this and what you want from me."

His green eyes darkened, his hand inching up until one finger brushed her labia, the light graze enough to send her arousal skyrocketing. Then again, all it had ever taken was one of his potent, focused looks to heighten her awareness and senses to the point of combustion.

"My job is to help you explore your needs and to push your boundaries so you can reach your full potential, and the rewards that come with submission."

She swallowed hard as he untied the robe with the hand at her waist and spread the sides to expose her. Unable to help herself, she looked down as he cupped her breast and thumbed her nipple, his skin so much darker than her pale flesh. The orange-and-black monarch butterfly tattoo with its wings spread to cover the side of her right breast drew his eye.

"I love this," he said, tracing the ink, "but I didn't like seeing Miller's hand on you, Amie, and I sure as hell don't care for the marks he left. If anyone is going to mark you, it'll be me, and you won't cringe from my hands on you."

"You sound so sure of that," Amie whispered, unable to keep from arching into his hand as he kneaded her breast.

"Now, if only I can be as sure of you," he murmured, leaning down and kissing her fast and hard. She couldn't look away when he lifted his head and slipped his finger between her labia, teasing the sensitive tissues until her legs slowly parted under his intense regard. "Excellent," he said, the one word enough to bolster her courage.

"Ben, Sir." Amie closed her eyes, forgetting about the people wandering around outside the cubicle and his obvious reluctance to believe she wasn't keeping some important secret from him.

It had only taken his hands on her again to lose herself in the new feelings he was good at producing. It didn't seem to matter whether his attention was in the form of a hard hand smacking her butt with stinging force or his fingers delving deep into her pussy, rasping her clit on the way. The result was the same – she went up in flames.

Ben pinched her nipple, sending a jolt through her already wired system, his voice low and guttural as he issued a two-word demand. "Tell me."

Recognizing that dominant, implacable tone, frustration whipped through Amie. She was burning with hunger for him and anything he wanted to do to her, but just as strong was a growing desire to be what *he* wanted. To get there, she needed him to just do, not ask.

"I don't know," she bit out. "That's your job."

The hard, stinging pinch to one tender fold went straight up her pussy, and she yelped from the surprise pain. "Ouch!" Before she could voice a complaint, an amused male voice came from the entrance into their secluded nook.

"I don't think she cared for your response to her tone, Master Ben."

Nick, the bartender, leaned against the hay stack, his mouth curled at the corners. Amie squirmed and reddened as he took in her nakedness with an appreciative lingering look, but adding to her embarrassment was the quick way her nipples puckered tighter under the other man's gaze.

Ben tightened his hand on her breast and pressed his palm between her legs, holding his finger inside her quivering sheath. "Then she should watch her tone."

Amie grew uncomfortable under their stares yet even hotter and needier from his compressed hold. The fervent desire to make Ben proud of her overrode both fierce reactions, and she uttered the first word that came to mind.

"Sorry."

Ben grinned. "That's the first time you've given an apology I wanted to hear." Glancing back up at Nick, he asked, "Everything okay out there?"

A look passed between the two, and Nick nodded. "Under control, and no other issues. I'll catch you later." He winked at Amie and walked off, leaving her to guess their exchange had something to do with Cal.

Pulling his finger slowly from her pussy, Ben asked, “Where were we?” He tickled her clit, tugged on the nub, then traced over her bare labia with his damp finger, every touch shortening her breath. “Oh yeah, you were reminding me of my job. Good enough.”

The rigid outline of his cock pressing against her buttocks was as heat-inducing as the objects he reached down and pulled from the black bag sitting unnoticed on the floor. The sight of his big hand holding the small, egg-shaped bullet vibrators attached by a short cord distracted her from the loss of his calloused finger toying with the sensitive tissues inside her pussy.

“I didn’t see the bag,” she said, unable to come up with anything else.

“Because I didn’t want to add to any nervousness you might be feeling. From your expression, I’m guessing you know what these are, or have used them before.” Setting the vibrators on her belly, he retrieved a tube of ointment next.

“I haven’t tried them but came across them, and others, when researching. You like toys?” She’d never been interested in exploring with anything other than her vibrator.

Until now. Since meeting Ben, a lot of new

things were suddenly appealing.

"Good. I like knowing I'm the first for you in some things."

Amie chuckled. "So long as *you're* not expecting to be my first."

Ben's gaze shot to her face, his eyes hot as he rumbled, "When *I'm* inside you, you won't think about anyone before me, and when I'm through, you won't remember them."

Oh, wow, that's a challenge I'll be happy to concede to him. "Okay, if you insist."

"I do. Spread your legs and lean back." Removing his arm from around her waist, he drew her hands behind her, holding them by the wrists at her lower back as he waited for her to lie against the chair's armrest.

Amie was surprised by how fast she'd grown comfortable sitting naked on Ben's lap with a room full of people mingling just yards away, and how easy it was to open her thighs without hesitation. If she were honest, this whole scene was a huge rush simply because she was the sole focus of Ben's attention.

She welcomed the return of his fingers delving into her pussy, moaning as he nestled the egg-shaped vibrator against the nerve endings inside her, her thighs tightening to contain the immediate spark of pleasure.

Goose bumps popped out watching him lube the attached bulb then slide his fingers between her buttocks, his gaze lifting to her flushed face. “Have you indulged in any anal play?” he inquired, pressing the toy against her anus.

Amie shook her head, wishing again he would just forge ahead. “No, but it’s fine. I’m good.” She caught the hint of frustration in her tone and clenched her hands behind her, holding her breath as he nudged the tight orifice again.

“I’m not going to risk your physical or emotional well-being for any reason, Amie, which is why I ask the necessary questions.” Another push and the bullet slid past the tight constriction. “You can breathe out now.”

Ignoring his amused tone, she released her pent-up breath, her whole body shuddering as he worked the small stimulator a little deeper before withdrawing his fingers and asking, “You good?”

She started to say fine, but the look on his face demanded honesty. “No, you’ve got me worked up yet keep pausing. It’s annoying.”

He grinned, and her heart stuttered. “I love it when you don’t hold back.”

Patting her thigh, he released her hands and helped her up. When she stood before him, wobbling, he gripped her hips, leaned forward, and suckled each nipple before grabbing her clothes and helping her dress.

"That's it? You're just going to leave me like this?" Amie didn't know whether to smack him or cuddle against him.

"No. I'm going to take you back to my place and give you what you want." Fisting her hair, he drew her up to kiss her hard and fast before adding against her trembling mouth, "What we both want."

****

Coincidence my ass.

Cal Miller released the girl's arms from the bondage chair with one eye on Amie Buchanon walking out the door with Wilkins. Just as he'd thought before he'd spotted Myla Norton's friend the other day, her presence in these parts had to be by design. The chit was as stupid as Myla if she thought she could get anything on him to take back home to the authorities.

"I'm done with you," was all he said to the sub who'd refused to allow anything except a light flogging. *Boring.*

Leaving her standing there, he also left the club, his mind off the disappointing scene and now focused on what fun he could have with Amie that wouldn't jeopardize his freedom.

Chapter Eight

Ben took a moment while Amie dressed to let Drew know he was leaving with her then flicked on the vibrators with the remote in his pocket as he ushered her out to his vehicle. Her breast-lifting indrawn breath tugged at his lips, her quick acceptance and responses thus far everything he could hope for. She possessed an appealing mix of sexual submissiveness and fierce refusal to let him, or anyone, he would guess, push her where she didn't want to go. That sweet blend drew him like a magnet, impossible to resist.

"Problem?" he asked. Opening his truck door, he saw the combined lust and frustration depicted on her rosy face.

"Other than you constantly catching me off guard, no. You're the one always insisting on verbal communication. Doesn't that go both ways?"

Lifting her onto the passenger seat, he flicked

her nose. "Not always. Buckle up." He shut the door on her frown, enjoying keeping her guessing and on edge. The reward when her orgasm sucked him dry would be worth her peevishness.

"That's not fair," she complained as soon as he slid behind the wheel after retrieving the remote from his pocket.

"Didn't anyone ever tell you life isn't fair?"

Those extraordinary bright eyes darkened with pain, and she turned her face toward the window. "I learned that at a young age without anyone saying."

Ben pulled out before reaching over and squeezing her clenched hand. "Care to talk about it?"

Her fast headshake sent her hair swinging around her neck and cheeks. "No."

"Then let's get back to more pleasant things."

Amie jerked with a low gasp as he upped the pulses teasing her orifices, the noticeable quivering of her body proof of how the tiny vibrations were affecting her. "What do you think of your new toys?"

She managed to get herself together enough to flash him a smile. "I think you'd better drive faster."

"Good enough."

More than, he thought, considering the discomfort of his raging erection crammed against his zipper. His place wasn't far, and by the time he pulled her inside the house, he wasn't sure he could hold back long enough to get to his bedroom.

"If you need the restroom, do it now while I see to the dogs," he instructed while trying to settle them down. Normally, he loved their enthusiastic welcome home, but not with a case of combustible lust riding him hard.

"I don't," she returned in a wobbly tone, leaning against the door.

Ben swore. "Don't move. Come on, guys." Hurrying into the kitchen, it took every ounce of his control to stick with their routine and give them a treat before returning to the living room where Amie hadn't budged.

Her eyes widened as he stalked toward her, and he was sure she read the intent on his face correctly. He made short work of stripping off her sweatshirt and yanking down her jeans. Without a word and with a desperate eagerness that matched his, she stepped out of the denim, kicking it aside as he pulled the silky camisole over her head. Instead of waiting on him, she shimmied out of the shorts, her breasts swaying with her efforts. Ben tweaked one nipple while loosening his jeans then pinned that soft body against the door.

His heart thudded as he braced his hands

against the door behind her. "Why does it seem like we've been headed here forever?" Instead of waiting for her to answer, he sank his teeth into her plump lower lip, relishing the tight clasp of her hands on his forearms.

"Ben, Sir, *please*."

The aching undertone lacing her plea got to him. Using one hand to knead a full breast, he slid the other between her legs and removed the vibrators. She whimpered, and he chuckled. He replaced them with his thumb in her pussy and middle finger in her ass, her cream and the lube making it easy to finger-fuck her with deep, penetrating thrusts. She mewled and gyrated against his hand, and he damn near whimpered.

"Now, Amie," he insisted in a harsh voice, releasing her breast to get a condom from his back pocket.

"Yes, yes, now."

Amie's rushed agreement blew across his cheek with her warm breath, both ramping up his expectations as he sheathed himself with one hand while continuing to work her pussy and ass. She surprised him when she shoved his hand off his cock and finished the task herself, her hot palm searing his flesh through the thin latex.

Amie huffed with impatience. "You're too slow."

"I'll take you to task for that complaint later," he rasped, not at all offended.

"Okay, much later though."

Wrapping a leg around his hip, she rode his pummeling hand with unabashed abandon he got off on watching before her slick walls convulsed around his thumb with the increased spurt of wet heat, signaling an end to waiting. He pulled from her clutching body, reached behind her, and grabbed her buttocks to lift her onto his cock.

"Hold on tight," he warned as she latched onto his shoulders with her hands, her other leg circling his hip until her feet crossed and her heels were digging into his lower back. "That's it, Amie. Now."

Ben speared her folds with the ease of a knife sliding through soft butter, her pussy wet, warm, and so fucking welcoming he saw stars with the first penetrating thrust. "*Fuck*!" he muttered, forcing himself to hold back.

Her giggle against his neck came close to undoing him. "I thought that was what we were doing. *Oh*!" she exclaimed on a gasp as he answered that smart-ass remark with three rapid, hard strokes that pushed her against the door.

"Shut up, Amie."

"Okay. Sorry."

He glared at her, and she giggled again until he slid a finger between her cheeks and teased the sensitive tissue of her anus. Leaning her head against the door, she closed her eyes, bit her lower lip, and shook with the force of his pummeling cock. He didn't have time to dwell on how much he loved that look as her pussy clamped around his shaft, the swollen muscles gripping his rigid length with tight suctions.

Dipping his head, Ben bit one turgid peak then soothed the sting with a stroke of his tongue. He started to do the same on the left, but Amie took that moment to climax, her soft cry and spasming pussy enough to release his own orgasm in a torrid flow of hot ecstasy. He rode through the pleasure with Amie's damp body straining against him, her moans mingling with his until the only sound in the room when his head cleared was their labored breathing.

"You okay, Amie?" he whispered in her ear, pulling slowly from her tight sheath.

"More than." She sighed, the sound drawing his smile.

"Good to know."

In one quick move, he hoisted her over his

shoulder, spun around, and strode down the hall to his bedroom. Tossing her on the bed, he eyed her bouncing breasts and the shiny evidence of her climax between her parted legs as he stripped off his clothes and the used condom.

With a wicked grin and a fist around his semi-erection, Ben asked, "Do you need anything before we begin round two?"

****

Amie quaked inside and out, eyeing his slow pumping hand gripping his jutting cock, her body still pulsing from their first go-around. "Round two already?" The man was a sex God, and, for tonight at least, all hers. How did she get so lucky?

"Again, are you good, or do you want to wait? Answer honestly, or you'll be sorry."

Her cheeks clenched from his serious, dark tone, but instead of the bare-butt-spanking threat turning her off, she went damp imagining the burning sting. Too bad she was on board with round two now.

"I'm good."

Without a word, he flipped her over and dragged her to her knees, leaving her shoulders and face pressed to the soft bed, her hips elevated. "Nice.

Your artwork surprises me and hints at your hidden depths." He traced the colorful butterflies adorning her lower back, each one right above her buttocks, then slid two fingers inside her and said with mock disappointment, "Damn. I was half hoping you were hedging again."

Ben didn't give her time to reply, replacing his fingers with his steely cock. The deep plunge pushed her forward before he yanked her back against his groin, held tight, and set up a steady pounding rhythm that sent her senses reeling all over again. Amie rode through the pleasure, losing track of time and place until she found herself sprawled on her back again, staring up at the ceiling, panting.

She didn't realize she was smiling until he returned from the bathroom and lay down next to her. Ben leaned up on one elbow and gazed down at her, his lips quirking up at the corners as he asked, "What's the grin for?"

Lifting a hand to touch him for the first time, she sifted her fingers through the crisp, black hair hairs sprinkled across his pecs. "I was thinking I should have listened to my best friend and indulged in a vacation fling before this. She was definitely on to something."

"It sounds like you two are close." Cupping her

breast, he ran an idle stroke over her nipple with his thumb, then another, and another.

"We are. She's the sibling I never had."

Bending his head, he licked her aching tip. "Tell me about her."

That surprised her. Given the trust involved in this kind of relationship, she understood his reasoning for wanting some personal information about her, but hearing about a friend back home didn't seem to fit there. Still, she found herself unable to deny him anything at that moment. Maybe she didn't want to lose the pleasant afterglow from the sex, his closeness, and his tender expression. If that was the case, she was happy to answer.

"We grew up together from toddlers, lived next door, went all through school and college glued to the hip. After college, we got separate apartments, jobs, and each have other friends, but none of that interfered with our bond. It's wonderful having someone who knows you so well, is aware of your faults and doesn't judge, is there for you through thick and thin, without question or fail."

A spasm of pain crossed his face, and she reached up to caress his taut, bristled jaw. "I'm sorry. Did I say something that bothers you?"

"No, not at all. You're lucky to have her."

A sudden shiver racked her, whether from her cooling body or his continued touch was up for grabs. Of course, he noticed, and it ruined her chance to ask him anything else.

"Up you go." Ben pulled her off the bed and swatted her butt, the sting eliciting a yelp of surprise. Palming the offended spot, he nudged her forward. "Take care of what you need to in the bathroom and get in bed. I'm beat."

Amie spun around in pleased surprise. "You want me to stay the night?"

One dark brow winged upward. "I'm sure as hell not driving you all the way back into town. Go."

Fighting back a giggle and the urge to do a little dance, she decided she didn't mind obeying some orders that weren't sex-related.

Amie came slowly awake, her nose twitching as she inhaled the rich aroma of brewing coffee the next morning. Rolling over in the big bed, she groaned as body aches from the night's excess made themselves known. Blinking against the bright sun streaming in through the window, she embraced the splash of warmth across her face and chest. Keeping her eyes half closed, she reached a hand across the bed but didn't encounter any of Ben's enticing, bulging muscles.

Bummer. I guess someone has to be making that coffee.

She slid out of bed and stumbled toward the bathroom, grabbing her lingerie set and the men's T-shirt Ben had left on a chair, his thoughtful gesture one more thing to like about him. If he kept revealing these nice quirks, she might not want to leave.

The plush gray carpet was soft and warm under her feet, much preferable to hardwood on a cool morning. Last night, she'd been focused on Ben and his intentions and had taken little notice of his room. Like the main room and kitchen, the bathroom's rustic charm appealed to her much more than an updated, modern look. The dark-green stained wood on the double-sink vanity was topped with a white marble countertop, the swirls of green and browns giving it a pop of color that tied in with the wood tile backsplash. The large walk-in shower's walls were covered in the same pattern, and a towel-warming rack stood next to the half-wall that left the stall open.

"Don't get used to this," Amie lectured herself after using the new toothbrush he'd left out for her then stepping into the shower and turning on the overhead rain showerhead.

She needed to call Myla today to remind herself why she couldn't let wishful thinking slip past her guard. Ben might have taken his duties as her temporary Dom past what was expected by bringing her home and letting her stay the night, but she wasn't gullible enough to believe she was the only woman to share his private space. She might wish she lived closer and could return often, but that wasn't feasible. Omaha was home, not Mountain Bend, no matter how much she liked the small town and the people.

Amie lingered under the hot spray for as long as she could without keeping Ben waiting too long. After drying with one of the heated towels, she decided she needed to get one of those warming racks when she got home. The silky lingerie felt as good against her sensitive skin as last night, but the soft, worn cotton of Ben's shirt that carried his scent was even better. She inhaled with renewed lust, as she padded out to the main room, wondering when she'd turned into such a sex maniac.

"Besides coffee, what smells so good?" she asked Ben as soon as she caught a whiff of whatever was in the oven.

Turning from the toaster, he eyed her bare legs and his shirt with a hot look before answering, "A breakfast casserole, my sister's recipe. Five more minutes. What do you like on your toast?"

"Just butter, thanks."

Amie found him working in the kitchen wearing nothing but jeans too distracting and wandered over to the stone fireplace. An eight-by-ten photo sat on the mantel, and she reached up to take it down and get a closer look at the young man who was the spitting image of Ben.

Pivoting, she held it up toward him from across the room. "Your brother?"

His mild expression hardened with his curt nod. "Yes. Put it back and come eat."

Touched a nerve, did I? Given his insistence for open dialogue without evasive answers, she wasn't about to let it drop there. Considering the placement of the photo, the close sibling resemblance that hinted they were twins, and his gruff tone, it was obvious Ben loved him. She returned the picture and joined him at the round kitchen table, her stomach rumbling as she eyed the bubbling egg, cheese, hashbrown, and sausage casserole.

"I might need that recipe," she said, sitting down across from him. While he scooped a serving on her plate, she asked again about his brother. "You look like twins. Does he live nearby?"

Ben lowered his fork and glared at her. "I don't wish to discuss my brother. Eat." He aimed his utensil at her raised hand holding a forkful of casserole.

Instead of obeying, she returned his glare with one of her own and lowered her hand. "So, if I had said that last night when you asked about Myla, you would have been fine with that?"

He grimaced then blew out a beath, tunneling his fingers through his hair, scooping it back. "Good point. I apologize."

Amie wasn't used to men apologizing, and the sincerity in his tone caught her by such surprise she almost dropped her fork. She managed to put it in her mouth, waiting for him to say something else, wanting to know more about him besides his sexual preferences.

"Bart died in a rodeo accident fifteen years ago." His sad green gaze shifted to the photo and lingered. "We were twins, very close, but he possessed a daredevil streak and attitude I didn't. I spent a good portion of our first twenty-one years rushing to his rescue and wasn't there for him only one time. But then, that's all it takes, isn't it?"

Her heart clenched, and the food lodged in her throat for a second, the guilt and painful memory etched on Ben's dark face hard to witness. Having suffered through Mike's suicide, she could empathize with Ben's pain but only to a certain degree. She'd loved Mike as a neighbor and friend, but she imagined Ben's feelings went as deep, or deeper than hers for Myla. She worked to swallow before saying, "I'm so sorry. I shouldn't have brought him up again. The food is delicious."

He shrugged. "You were right to point out my hypocrisy in expecting openness from you and then denying you the same respect. I'm not used to someone exposing my flaws, but I'll try to do better from here on out."

Her pulse took a flying leap at that statement, his announcement he wanted to continue seeing her while she was here. She sipped her coffee before answering, getting herself under control so as not to sound so needy and pleased over keeping his attention for longer.

"I kinda like your bossiness at the club and last night in your bedroom," she admitted with a teasing glance. "And I never imagined I would go for such a thing, not with the men I've known."

Ben cocked his head, regarding her with a direct stare as he chewed before answering that bald confession. "A little advice, babe. Don't mention other men to me."

Oooh, jealousy? If so, I like it – way too much.

Pushing that possibility aside, Amie realized that was the first time he used a generic endearment with her, and she didn't like it. Call the tight knot in her abdomen envy, she didn't care, regardless that was an ill-advised emotion considering their circumstances.

"Okay," she returned coolly, "if you can keep from calling me babe." She left it at that instead of adding other pet names that would also annoy her. That would give too much away, and she would be returning home with enough emotional baggage to sort through without leaving him knowing she had developed a possessive jealousy toward him.

His lips tilted, drawing her eyes to his mouth, stirring up memories of those lips tugging on her nipples and suckling the sting when he would nip the tender skin on her neck. He must have read something of her sudden aroused longing on her face as he said, "I can do that. Finish up and we'll go for a ride before I take you home."

Pushing his chair back, he picked up his plate and carried it to the sink, leaving her to stare at his broad back while trying to rein in her excited expectation. Amazing how, with a few words, he could get her juices flowing and her blood pumping in a heated rush. Then she remembered her lack of clothes.

"Um, thanks, but I don't have anything to wear riding, remember?"

Turning from the sink, he said, "My sister has some things in the spare room, and you two are close to the same size. You finish the dishes while I go see what'll work. I didn't think to make that offer when you were here yesterday."

"That's okay. I'll take you up on it today. Thanks."

Giddiness assailed her as she swallowed the last few bites watching the dogs follow at his heels down the hall, their attachment to their rescuer obvious in many little ways. As it turned out, he was a good judge of women's sizes, the jeans, hoodie, and boots he loaned her fitting close to perfect.

Amie met Ben at the back door, ready for whatever he had planned, both today and during the remainder of her stay in Mountain Bend. Her only concerns going forward were her ability to shield her heart and avoiding any more contact with Cal Miller.

Shouldn't be too difficult, right?

****

Cal grinned as he watched Wilcox come out of his house with the Buchanon girl. After seeing them leave together last night, he'd banked on finding them together at Wilcox's place. He'd planted himself in the same spot as last time early this morning, and his patience had paid off. They entered the stable and exited ten minutes later with Wilcox leading two horses.

"Oh yeah, never waste a chance to cop a feel," he said aloud as Wilcox boosted Amie up into the saddle on the small mare with a hand on her ass.

She appeared comfortable on a horse but not as at ease as the ranger. Yeah, he'd done his homework and checked the guy out. He needed to know how far he could go with turning the tables on Norton's little friend, and decided the risks were well worth the fun of watching her squirm for a few days. Besides, what was life without risks?

He kept the binoculars on the couple as they rode across the pastureland, waiting until he was sure of their direction before hopping on his ATV and following their path north. Odds were Wilcox was taking her to the lake at the base of Quail Ridge. "Damn, I'm good," he congratulated himself, peering through the trees and seeing the couple had already arrived. Other than a pair of older fishermen out in a boat, there was no one else around, so it didn't surprise him when Wilcox pointed toward the wide trail Cal was on and they headed his way.

Spinning around, Cal drove out to a clearing then south far enough to leave the ATV and circle back through the dense forest on foot. As soon as he heard their voices, he crouched, moving with caution and stealth until he caught sight of them by a large Douglas fir. Wilcox must not have gotten his fill last night as his voice filtered back to Cal who eyed the other Dom turning Amie to face the tree. Placing her hands against the rough bark, he yanked her jeans down.

"Fast and hard, so brace yourself, Amie."

"Okay."

Her voice, soft and breathless with excitement, got Cal's arousal stirring. Wilcox wasn't kidding as he wasted no time suiting up, kicking her feet apart, and thrusting into her cunt. Wilcox's smacks on her white ass echoed through the trees, along with their panting grunts. Cal imagined taking a thick tree branch to those soft buttocks. Walloping the tender flesh a good long while and drawing a little blood would suit him just fine. One of his fondest memories of Mike had been when the kid, in his eagerness to please him, had let him beat his ass with a crop.

Man, he'd enjoyed that night, reaming his ass with the beads of bright red blood sliding down his crack.

Too bad the kid had gone and blown their perfect relationship by falling in love with him. In all these years, he'd never found a guy or girl as malleable as young Mike, forcing him to limit his sadistic needs to hunting.

Speaking of which – if he wanted to leave a surprise for the couple to return and find, he'd better hightail it back now. When Wilcox said fast, he wasn't exaggerating. Cal crept back to the ATV and went hunting for prey.

Chapter Nine

Ben couldn't recall when he had enjoyed a leisure afternoon ride more. After he'd given Amie a few pointers, she'd handled Destiny without a problem, the same way she'd ridden the gentle mount he'd chosen for her on the trail ride. The dainty mare had come to him last year after her rescue from a farm in Montana. She was only one of over thirty malnourished horses that were re-homed at the owners' request when they finally realized they were in over their heads and, despite their good intentions, couldn't give the herd the care they required. Destiny was the perfect size and temperament for Amie, but her small stature meant a slower pace so the mare could keep up with Thunder's longer legs. Next time, he would take her up with him and let her experience racing across the range. There was nothing like an exuberant ride with the wind on your face and a powerful animal under you.

"You had a good time," he stated when the stable and corrals came into view.

"I did." Amie whipped her head toward him, grinning, the move sending her sun-streaked light brown hair flying around her neck and cheeks, the layered cut keeping it from getting in her way. "All of it."

"Good to know."

Ben hadn't intended to drag her into the woods for sex, but her curiosity about the land had pleased him, her laugh had drawn his own, and the smile she couldn't seem to lose was as potent as the strongest aphrodisiac. He liked spending time with her way too much for someone who was here visiting.

Just as he spotted what looked like a deer carcass lying between the stable and corral, Amie announced, "Let's end it with a bang. Race you!"

She nudged Destiny into a gallop before he could stop her. "Amie, wait!" he thundered, going after her. From what he could see, the carcass would shock her, and that pissed him off as much as the deliberate placement of the dead animal on his property.

He managed to head her off as she reached the fence line, Thunder forcing

Destiny to veer left instead of riding right up to the deer. Unfortunately, Amie got a glimpse of the gutted doe, her face going sheet white as they both reined their horses to a halt. Her bright eyes were swimming with tears as she jumped down with a choked sob, bent over, and threw up her breakfast.

Swearing, Ben dismounted and pulled a handkerchief from his pocket, wet it in the water trough, and handed it to her. "Here. This will help." He put his arm around her as she straightened and took the cloth with shaking fingers.

"Who...sorry, who would do...such a thing?"

"I don't know, but don't fucking apologize for being human. I'm sickened also, and I've seen worse. Come on. I'll help you inside then deal with this." Starting with calling Shawn out here, his fury at the deliberate surprise tightening every muscle. He wondered if the hunter they were searching for had gotten wind of the rangers' intention to find and stop him and this was delivered as a threat. If so, the son of a bitch didn't know who he was messing with.

Her easy compliance hinted at her vulnerable state, adding to the rage pounding at him. He shielded her from seeing the deer again as he ushered her past it and into the house. The dogs were there, circling her with tails wagging, and she went to her knees to hug and pet them.

"I'm okay, Ben," she mumbled into Sheba's neck. "Go do what needs to be done."

He reached down and ran a hand over her hair then stormed back outside. Pressing Shawn's number on his cell, he studied the carcass, waiting for the sheriff to answer. From the amount of blood around the bullet hole, the deer had been dead before the bastard had taken a knife and opened its gut. The quick, painless death added to his theory this was left as either a threat or some sick joke, and he wasn't laughing.

"What's up, Ben?" Shawn asked.

"I need you at my place ASAP." He didn't care if he was abrupt and demanding, not with Amie's stricken face etched in his brain. After giving him a brief rundown, he added, "If Dakota is available, I could use his help also."

"Both he and Clayton are here. We're on our way. The girls can sit with Amie."

"Make sure you instruct them to stay inside, and thanks."

Ben returned to the house to wait, in need of a stiff drink before he cleaned up the mess. Even with the help coming, it was going to be an unpleasant end to the enjoyable day.

Amie looked up from her position on the floor where she still sat petting the dogs. Reaching up, she took the glass Ben handed her and shot down the splash of potent whiskey in one fiery gulp. He saw on her face when the liquor hit her empty stomach with a punch, and her shudder against its impact.

"Thanks, I think," she choked, handing him back the glass.

"You're welcome." Crouching down, he nudged her chin up with two fingers. "I'm sorry. I've hunted and seen more than one animal-eaten carcass, and yet, some things are still intolerable. The deer was shot dead before being gutted if that helps."

"Yeah, it does. Thinking of it suffering was the worst. You're so lucky to have these guys." She smiled at Shadow, the black lab mix, when he licked her hand. Rubbing behind his ears, she crooned, "You're a good boy, aren't you?"

He stood and held out his hand as the dogs dashed to the front door, barking at the sound of cars pulling up out front. "That'll be the sheriff, Dakota, and Clayton. The girls are with them."

Heat enveloped her face. "Excuse me a minute, then, while I use the restroom."

Even with the whiskey coating her mouth, he imagined she still needed to refresh her mouth from hurling outside. "Go ahead. I'll head outside, but you girls stay in."

"You don't need to use your Dom tone with that order. I'm only too happy to stay here."

Amie could hear the others entering the house as she reached Ben's bathroom. She hurried to splash her face with cold water, which helped put color back into her cheeks, then brushed her teeth. Lisa, Poppy, and Skye's sympathetic greeting when she returned to the living room brought tears to her eyes again.

"How awful for you!" Lisa exclaimed, giving her a hug.

"Don't worry, Amie. Dakota will make mincemeat of the bastard when they find him," Poppy vowed. "I plan to cheer him on, when the time comes."

"I'll join you," Amie said.

Skye moved in to take Lisa's place hugging her, and Amie developed a serious case of fan meltdown. She couldn't believe how down-to-earth and nice she was, considering she was practically a celebrity, at least in Amie's eyes.

"If tying one on will help, we'll join you. I would have given anything if I had someone to go on a binge with after waking with no memory to my husband's murdered body." Skye stepped back, shivering.

Sympathy and guilt assailed Amie. A mutilated animal carcass was nothing compared to that. "I'm so sorry. Puking over an animal seems so ridiculous compared to what you went through."

"Oh, good grief, we all need a drink after that silly comparison. Amie, there's nothing trivial about coming across an animal with its entire insides spilled on the ground. Gross." Poppy wrinkled her nose as she stepped behind the small corner bar and checked the contents underneath. "All the hard stuff, but I prefer a beer. You guys?"

"Let's raid his refrigerator for beers, and I can

go for a snack," Lisa suggested.

Amie stood back and watched Lisa pull four beers from Ben's refrigerator, envying the way the three of them were comfortable making themselves at home in Ben's house. Granted, they had known him for months as opposed to two weeks for her. She wished she could stay a lot longer, or lived closer, as she'd like to get to know them and Ben better. But she missed home, and Myla, and cultivating friendships here wouldn't change that.

By the time the guys came back in over an hour later, all four wearing tight, grim expressions, Amie had a buzz going. The girls had regaled her with tales of their submissive experiences. Their lustful satisfied sighs and the images they'd put in her head were enough to turn her thoughts off the deer and onto Ben and herself. All it took for her blood to start pumping in a rapid torrent of pulsing heat through her body was one emerald-green searing glance as he removed his Stetson.

Her increasing lust and need for him should have started tapering off by now, she thought, since her body was still humming from his rough possession in the woods. That heady fucking should have lasted her a day or two, at the least, but here she was, pining for more with an ache that wouldn't go away.

Dakota scowled and plucked Poppy's beer out of her hand. "Time to go."

Amie watched Poppy stand and take Dakota's hand without arguing, figuring the redhead knew when to push and when to go along. She said goodbye to everyone after accepting an invitation to lunch on Wednesday when schools were closing early for conferences and Lisa could join them. The emotional exhaustion etched on Ben's tanned face cooled her libido and cleared her head, so she rose from his comfy sofa and offered a reassuring smile.

"I'll change out of your sister's clothes if you're ready to drive me back to the B&B."

Ben nodded. "I have to go into the office this evening and fill out a report to save time tomorrow, but we can stop for a burger. You must be hungry."

"Yes, thanks." She wasn't sure her stomach was ready for food, but she needed to eat and didn't want the weekend to end.

There was nothing but work and a call to Myla waiting for her at the Miner's Junction inn though. At one time, right before coming here, that had been enough for Amie. She was sure it would be again once she arrived home and settled back into her routine without the constant distraction of her Dom cowboy.

An hour later, Amie was leaning against the pillows stacked behind her on the bed, her phone to her ear, grinning as Myla insisted, "Tell me everything, in detail."

It was so good to hear the return of Myla's chipper voice without the stuttering. "I don't think I should go into too much detail," she teased. "Since you're still in rehab, I don't want you worked up with no way to get relief."

"Well...as it turns out, Matt has an inventive streak I can get used to, but that's all I'm saying until you spill."

That was enough incentive for Amie, and she told Myla everything, starting when she first met Ben at the Sunday buffet. "I admit, there's something to this kink, but for me, it's more the man than anything else."

"He's that hot, huh?"

"Yes, but more than the whole rugged, cowboy Dom thing he has going on in spades. He rescues animals, which I like, and keeps insisting I reveal every thought, which gets annoying but since no other guy has cared enough to show such interest, I tolerate that flaw." Amie wondered if she would miss that about him when she left and hoped not.

There were already too many traits she was going to have trouble forgetting.

Myla's laugh resonated in her ear. "Girlfriend, you have it bad, but we'll get back to that. What aren't you telling me? It's something to do with Miller, isn't it?"

Amie blew out a breath and leaned her head back. What made her think she could hide anything from her, even over the phone? They knew each other too well for that. "Yes. He's as much an ass as we thought, and I've no doubt capable of running you off the road and driving away without remorse. He's downright scary, Myla."

"Damn it, Amie, I told you to forget that plan of yours! I never should have mentioned you helping me, but you should have listened when I retracted my plea."

"I know, I know, and trust me, I'm not going near him again. He hooked up with a girl after I had a short conversation with him at the bar. Finding out he's bi means I dodged a bullet there, too. I wondered why he tried to push me into doing a scene with him."

"I never gave it much thought after Mike died. You promise me you're not going to push him if you see him again before leaving?"

Why did Amie keep experiencing that twinge in her chest whenever the word leaving came up? If it was due to her infatuation with Ben, she needed to get over it soon.

"Don't worry. I doubt I'll see him again. Ben and the club owners weren't pleased with him, and he didn't care for their attitudes. Since the club is the only place we have in common, I'm safe from him. Which is good because I want to hang around for a little while. Spurs is hosting a fundraiser game night that sounds like fun."

"Okay, but I'll expect you home after that, and more details. I'm hoping to get released this week, so we'll have lots to celebrate."

"And you've decided to leave Miller up to the cops?" Amie asked skeptically. After all this time and the lengths Myla had gone to, she found that hard to believe.

"I don't want to, but what choice do I have? The accident was a wake-up call for me, Amie. Between my struggles to recover and the worry I've caused my parents, I'm done."

"We won't let the cops give up, Myla. Call me when you're released. If you need me, I'll be there."

"No, stay, enjoy your guy. Matt's offered to stay at my place, and I took him up on it, so I don't have to impose on my mom and dad. Love you – bye!"

That was typical of Myla, ending their conversation abruptly after dropping a bombshell. She'd never known her friend to live with a guy, in fact, Myla had expressed her preference for living alone over and over since they'd graduated college. Amie was happy for her, glad Myla planned to do more than give Matt a chance by embracing a committed relationship. Regardless of the envious knot in her stomach, she wanted things to work out for her best friend. Having Matt around would help keep Myla's mind on him instead of dwelling on revenge for her brother's death.

Amie fell asleep dreaming what it would be like living in Ben's house with him and his animals but woke up missing Myla, her parents, and home.

She spent Monday working after breakfast, not venturing out until late afternoon when hunger pangs insisted she eat again. Hattie's Deli offered great sandwiches, and she'd already sampled the roast beef, but this time she craved soup. The bell tinkled as she entered, and Hattie beamed at her from behind the counter.

"Welcome back. Amie, right?"

The region around her heart grew warm. None of the employees at her favorite eating-out places back home had ever greeted her by name upon returning, not even after becoming a regular.

"Yes," she answered, walking up to the counter. Other than two couples occupying two tables, there were no other customers.

"Would you like the roast beef again or something else? Barbeque chicken is today's special."

The bell over the door jingled again, signaling another patron as Amie replied, "I'd planned on soup, but how about the pick two? I'll have a half of a chicken sandwich with the cheddar broccoli soup. That sounds good."

"I've had the soup and can vouch for it."

Amie went cold, every muscle tightening as she shifted away from Cal Miller who pressed next to her. Hattie narrowed her eyes, glancing between them, her mouth turning down in a frown.

"Sir, if you'll grab a seat, I'll take your order in a minute."

"That all right. I don't mind waiting next to this pretty lady. Ms. Buchanon and I have met."

He reached up and squeezed Amie's shoulder, hard. Gritting her teeth, she vowed not to let him get to her. "I'll eat here, Hattie." No way did she want him following her out.

"I'll join you," he said. "And get me the same,

please."

Incensed now, she rounded on him and stated loud enough for everyone to hear, "No, thank you. I don't want your company."

Hattie nodded, a small grin erasing her frown. "So, to go for your order?" she asked Miller in a sugary-sweet voice.

"Yes," he returned, appearing unperturbed by Amie's rebuke.

Going to the closest table, she sat down with her back to the counter and Miller, holding her breath until he left carrying a bag and Hattie served her order.

"I noticed something off about that guy the first time he came in. It's in his eyes. They lack warmth."

"He's a jerk." There was no way she would mention meeting him at Spurs. She doubted there were many Mountain Bend residents still unaware of the private club, but that didn't mean she was comfortable disclosing her visits. "We bumped into each other one day and discovered we were both from Omaha, but like you said, he gave off bad vibes, making me uncomfortable, and I didn't linger."

"Good. He s you any more trouble like I just saw, you tell our sheriff. Shawn will take care of him," Hattie stated with confidence.

"I've no doubt. Thanks, Hattie. This looks delicious."

The food was as good as it smelled, and Amie devoured it all, including the brownie Hattie added without charge. On Tuesday, after getting a call from Ben to tell her good morning and that he would be tied up with tracking down whoever had left the deer carcass until after dark all week, or until they found the culprit, she ordered seafood Alfredo from the B&B's kitchen.

Amie entered the dining room as Jen exited the kitchen carrying two steaming plates.

"I hope you don't mind me joining you," Jen said. "Tonight is Drew's poker night with friends from high school."

"Not at all, I'd love the company." Taking a seat, she added, "I think it's great they've kept in touch all these years. I have my best friend, who I've known since we were toddlers, but no one else of longevity."

Jen placed her plate in front of her then sat down with her same entrée. "I still get together with three of my closest friends from high school, but I meet them in Boise, where they now live. None of them are into the lifestyle, so it can get tricky balancing those friendships with the friends I have here who belong to the club."

"You have to watch what you say, I imagine." Amie took a bite of the creamy pasta and hummed with pleasure. "*Mmmm*, good."

"It's one of my favorites. Speaking of the club, I hear a Dom got pushy. I'm sorry. Sometimes the guests visiting as tourists or hunters can get out of hand as the guys don't have much time to wait on references. Drew said Clayton suggested no more passes to anyone not thoroughly checked out, regardless of how long they planned to stay here."

"I hate to be the one responsible for anything like that." She thought of Cal, and her part in drawing his attention, and his ire. It wouldn't be fair for her actions to bring about changes in their policy. "He didn't mean to come across so strongly, I'm sure." Which was a lie but for a good reason – to atone for her guilt in the matter.

Jen aimed her fork at her. "It doesn't

matter. Any Dom worth the title knows better. Don't make excuses for him."

Given their short acquaintance, Jen's unwavering support gave Amie a warm fuzzy feeling, the same as Hattie's yesterday. "I'm still new to everything. That's my excuse, and I'll stick with that and change the subject. Can you join me, Lisa, Poppy, and Skye for lunch tomorrow?"

"You bet. I rearranged my schedule after talking to Poppy. I told them you could ride with me, and we'll meet them at the Watering Hole. Like most bars, they have great food."

"That works for me. This was really good. Thanks for joining me, but I've got to return a library book and get back to call my parents this evening." She injected a rueful note in her voice as she admitted, "I'm an only child, and they worry."

"You're a good daughter, then. Enjoy your evening, and I'll see you tomorrow."

The compliment added a spring to Amie's step as she strolled out to her car. She planned to start Skye's new suspense tonight after returning the library book and visiting with her mom and dad. Driving to the library, her thoughts switched to Ben and his hunt for the bastard who made the mistake of leaving that deer on his property. She shuddered to think if he'd gotten hold of one of the llamas or horses and was glad Ben didn't leave them out unless he or his hired hand were around.

Amie parked out front, ran inside the library, and slid the book into the return slot then left before anyone could engage her in conversation. Not that she minded the friendliness of everyone, but she still had work to finish after calling home. As soon as she stepped outside, Cal's mocking voice came from behind her, sending shivers down her spine.

"No one around today to rush to your defense?"

She spun around and saw him leaning against the building, an insolent expression on his craggy face. "Are you following me?" Just asking produced a ball of nausea in her throat.

Pushing away from the building, he strode toward her with a taunting smile that gave her cold chills. She backed up until she bumped her car, and he pinned her there with his body, bracing his hands on the hood behind her.

"I'm not the one who followed you here from Omaha, you came after me, but you made a mistake, little girl."

With an abruptness that stole her breath, Cal stepped away from her with a ridiculing two-fingered salute. "See you later, Amie."

"If you keep harassing me, I'm going to the sheriff," she threatened even though Cal scared the crap out of her.

Looking back at her, he cocked his head and asked, "And tell him what, exactly? That you came here to stalk *me*?" Her surprise must have shone on her face because he chuckled and said, "It wasn't that hard to figure out, especially after your friend tried the same thing back home."

"You ran her off the road." Amie had no idea where her bravado came from, only that her anger was stronger than her fear.

"Prove it." He stalked off down the street without looking back.

Amie's skittering nerves stayed with her all night as she went over her options on what to do. The best thing, the smart course was to tell Ben and the sheriff everything, but Cal hadn't backed down after both men confronted him Saturday night, and her threat hadn't fazed him in the least. Besides, he was right about her following him here to stalk him.

She would start watching for him, avoid him if she spotted him anywhere near her, or just stay at the inn until she left with someone. Ben was so busy trying to track that sadistic hunter, she didn't want to burden him with her problem, not when she was leaving soon. There was the option of returning home now, but when she thought of missing out on more time with Ben and her new friends, an ache settled in her stomach and wouldn't go away. He was her one and only chance to explore more of the BDSM lifestyle she'd never imagined was for her, since she couldn't picture herself submitting to anyone but him, not any time soon.

Amie found herself wavering over her decision not to bother Ben when she saw Cal at the Watering Hole the next day after excusing herself from her friends to use the restroom. As she entered the short, dark hall where the restrooms were located, he came up behind her again and whispered in her ear.

"Be careful you don't drink too much, little girl. Your friend did, and ended up in an accident."

He continued out the back door without glancing around at her, leaving her standing there, shaken at the veiled threat. She'd watched for him on the drive here and had checked out the other tables when she'd wound her way toward the corner booth reserved for them. His stealthy hunting skills were proving beneficial for him, detrimental for her.

Dashing into the restroom, she splashed cold water on her face and worked to get herself under control before rejoining her friends. It wouldn't do for them to suspect something was wrong.

She hadn't counted on their significant others' astuteness wearing off on them.

"What's wrong, Amie?" Poppy demanded to know as soon as she returned and took her seat.

"Nothing. Why?" She avoided direct eye contact, instead giving her attention to finishing the chef salad in front of her.

"Because your hand is shaking, and your face is pale. Do you feel okay?" Skye asked.

Tears pricked Amie's eyes. They were being so nice, and she couldn't repay their kindness with lies. "To be honest, no." She looked up and around the table at their concerned faces. "Remember the Dom at Spurs who got too pushy?"

At their nods, she proceeded to tell them of Cal's stalking the last three days. "He'll tire of whatever game he's playing. It's just annoying, and a little creepy."

"You need to tell Ben and Shawn," Lisa insisted, and the others agreed.

She couldn't admit to threatening Miller with going to the sheriff without revealing his response of her starting it by following him here. She didn't want to leave on a sour note with these people after their friendly welcome into their small circle and into the club. If they learned she'd wanted the guest pass to find Miller and set him up to slip about harming either Mike or Myla, they'd likely not take that confession well.

One more week was all she desired before going home. Amie really wanted to attend game night at the club with Ben without burdening him or risking turning him away before then with the problem she'd created by her foolish plan.

"I will," she promised. "But only if he doesn't quit harassing me in the next day or two. They're so busy trying to track that abusive hunter that I don't want to interfere. Catching that guy is more important, especially if Miller gets bored antagonizing me soon."

"I don't know," Jen said. "I'm sure they can handle both issues just fine."

"And, speaking from experience, stalkers don't

give up. Don't wait too long." Lisa's green eyes clouded with bad memories.

Amie felt bad for resurrecting them, but all she said was, "Thanks, all of you."

Chapter Ten

Ben pulled up in front of the B&B and sat for a moment before going inside. He didn't know if he was more worried or pissed after hearing about Cal Miller harassing Amie. The last four nights he'd fallen into bed late, exhausted from tracking hours after his shift ended, Dakota's expertise coming in handy but still leading to dead ends. They questioned campers and hunting groups, but no one had heard or seen anything that would point to a certain person they could check out. At least there were no new maimed animals, that they knew of, and no more surprises waiting for him on his property. He still went to extra lengths to keep his animals safe, locking them in the barn whenever he or Joaquin weren't around.

The hardest part, he'd discovered, was having no time to spend with Amie. He called her every night after spending all day unable to quit thinking about her. Dakota and Neil ribbed him over it, his preoccupation noticeable to his two astute friends. Their teasing didn't bother him, but Amie's silence on Miller ticked him off. He understood she was leaving soon and likely thought it wouldn't matter in the long run.

But it did, damn it, at least, to him.

She was his responsibility while here, one he hadn't regretted agreeing to accept, and he shouldn't have heard about this trouble via Lisa's having told Shawn. Not only had he stressed the importance of honest openness between them, he liked her, more than liked if he were honest. Given his volatile reaction when Shawn relayed Lisa's concerns, he'd say he was as close to the L word than ever before with anyone else. If it weren't for the fact they resided in different states, he would welcome the possibility.

"Why can't anything be easy," he muttered, sliding out of his cruiser.

Regardless of feelings or distances, Amie should have come to him the first time Miller approached her outside the club. If they were going to continue together until she left, he needed to set her straight on a few things. He'd called Drew and asked if he could stop by this late, and after Drew assured him it was fine and that Amie was in, he headed that way.

The inn was locked at ten, their guests given a key to the rear door where they parked to use until they checked out.

Drew came out of his office when Ben entered, setting off the bell. “You can go on up. I’ll lock it again and it will automatically lock when you close it behind you. That way, if you decide to stay the night, it’ll be secure.”

“Thanks, Drew. I’m of a mind to drag her back to my place though. If that’s the case, I’ll leave you a note.”

“Good enough. I heard about Miller. That guy is bad news.”

“All the way around, but don’t worry about Amie. I’ll take care of her.”

Ben took the stairs up, ignoring Drew’s taunting gaze following him, hoping the creaks didn’t wake the other guests. He rapped on Amie’s door, his cock jerking when she opened it wearing nothing but a look of pleased surprise, and a thigh-skimming, sheer nightshirt with scooped neckline and capped sleeves.

Her bare toes curled into the carpet, her nipples turning rigid as she exclaimed in a soft voice, “Ben! What are you doing here so late?”

“Miller.”

She blanched and paled but stepped back to let him inside.

"Why didn't you tell me?" he demanded as soon as she closed the door and he crowded her against it. He braced his hands behind her, watching the wheels turning as she tried to come up with an answer.

"It wasn't a big deal, and I handled it, him."

"Try looking at me when you say that. You *might* sound more convincing."

Those extraordinary eyes flashed up at him, her soft mouth going taut. "Where in the rules does it say I have to run to you with every little problem?"

"Nowhere, but it's damn sure implied you need to come clean about big problems, like getting harassed by a Dom who has already left marks on you." He picked up her arm and showed her the fading bruises Miller left the other night. "Does your deliberate neglect in telling me about this threat mean you don't want to continue with me for the remainder of your stay?"

The instant denial and panic on her face sent a wave of satisfaction through Ben. Thank God for her open, expressive face. She shifted with uncertainty, her teeth worrying her lower lip.

"Answer me," he insisted, not letting her off the

hook. He needed the words.

Her deep breath lifted her breasts, then she exhaled, quaking. "No, I want to continue being with you. I'm sorry. I didn't think it was a big deal."

"Yes, you did, otherwise, you wouldn't have hesitated to tell me." He swung his head around, spotted her wooden-handled hairbrush on the nightstand, then peered down at her again. "The safewords are the same here, remember that."

Amie's eyes flared with heat and a hint of unease until he dropped to one knee and trailed his fingers up her inner thigh. "I accept your apology, but I'm still unhappy with you." Sliding his hands under the sleep garment, he kept his eyes on her face as he slid her panties down and she kicked them aside with an increase in her breathing.

"*Oh!* I...I thought you were mad," she gasped as he lifted one leg over his shoulder and licked his way up her other thigh.

"I am."

Ben swiped his tongue through her damp folds, her cream coating his tongue as he teased her clit. Circling the hard nubbin, he slid his middle finger deep inside her slick pussy, the tight clutch of her muscles a sign of her need.

Perfect.

Using his teeth, he tugged on her clit, soothed the discomfort with a lick, then pulled away and stood. "I'll finish what I started, or not, after your punishment."

Grabbing her hand, he pulled her over to the bed as she stuttered, "That's just plain...mean." She ended on a huff when he sat down and yanked her over his lap.

"I do what I have to do to drive my point home." He palmed her thigh then glided upward, lifting the nightshirt to her waist, baring her ass and the twin butterfly tattoos above each cheek. Tracing over the right one with a finger, he whispered, "These are so fucking sexy."

"Is that supposed to appease me?" she grumbled.

"I'm not here to appease you." Ben swatted first one buttock then the other. "It's my job to look after you." Two more spanks that bounced her cheeks. "And I can't do that if you keep things from me."

"I wasn't in danger. He approached me in public, for God's sake...*ouch*!"

Ben rubbed the center of her buttocks where he'd landed the last swat. "Can you imagine what it was like hearing about it from Shawn after Lisa told him? And they only found out because you have the type of face that shows everything you're feeling." He picked up the brush and ran the smooth back over her pink ass to distract her.

****

Amie whipped her head up and around and watched Ben hold up her brush before turning it in his hand and bringing it down on her butt. Pain blossomed and spread to cover her entire cheek, wrenching a moan from her clogged throat.

"Do you want to use the safe word?"

Narrowing her eyes at his taunting tone, she shook her head then flipped her facedown. "No, go ahead."

She refused to give in, to let him think she couldn't handle whatever he dished out. Besides, her clit still pulsed with need from the small amount of attention he'd given it, and she craved release more than she dreaded the brush. She jumped when he spanked the other cheek but bit her lip to keep from protesting as she quivered inside and out. The pleasure she'd reaped from lying over his lap and the trace of his calloused finger across her tattoo evaporated with the next two swats, the heated pain morphing into throbbing numbness with the final smacks.

Amie's muscles rippled as Ben caressed her abused backside, the soothing strokes helping her relax even though they did nothing to ease the discomfort of her hot, aching flesh. When he turned her over and cuddled her against his broad chest, pressing her head to rest with her ear against his heart's steady thumping, her eyes watered from keeping him in the dark about Cal's intimidation tactics. She had to admit he'd shown nothing but patience with her.

She opened her mouth to tell him the full reason she'd come to Idaho, but before she could utter a word, he twisted and laid her on the bed. With a wicked gleam in his eyes, he slid down her body, lifted her legs over his shoulders, and put his mouth on her again.

One swipe of his tongue between her labia sent her hips straining against his mouth and stripped her head of all coherent thought as she exclaimed, "*Ben*!"

Ignoring her strident cry, he delved inside her pussy with tongue and fingers, his five-o'clock beard scratchy against her inner thighs. He nipped her thrumming clit, and she gasped from the instant heat; he soothed the pinprick with a soft lick, and she moaned from the pleasurable ripples; he thrust hard and deep, and she jerked with the pressure against sensitive tissues; and then he suckled her aching nub until she whimpered from the small contractions heralding a climax. Seconds before her body erupted with an explosive orgasm, he pulled back and stood, fisting his hands on his hips, her cream glistening on his lips, a hard set to his mouth that didn't bode well for what he had to say.

"I've decided you can wait until Friday for an orgasm. The delay will help you think twice about keeping something so important from me again."

Incensed, Amie's decision to tell him everything went out the window as she sat up, yanking the nightshirt down. "That's not fair. You said if I accepted my punishment..."

Ben held up a hand, forestalling her tirade. "This is part of your punishment. Deal with it. This time, your omission could have landed you in trouble."

He was right, and she didn't like that anymore than she enjoyed sitting there with her body on fire, pulsating for release, so she lashed out. "Leave. Now."

With a shrug that hurt her feelings, he pivoted and strode to the door. Pausing with a hand on the knob, he turned his head around to deliver a parting shot that caused her heart to execute a slow roll.

"I care enough about you to incur your anger, and possibly your future rejection if it ensures your safety. Lock the door after me."

"Well, hell, why'd he have to go and say that?"

She rose and flipped the lock then shut the lamp off and crawled into bed wishing she'd called him back. Masturbating would take care of her pressing need, but she ached for Ben, not her hand.

****

This is almost too easy.

Cal watched Wilcox leave the bed-and-breakfast, thinking his timing was fucking perfect. The run-in with the Buchanon girl at the deli had been by pure chance but had given him the idea of stalking her around town. The next day, he'd staked out the B&B in the late afternoon and eaten a hamburger in his Jeep while waiting to see if she ventured out, since her car was in the rear parking lot. He'd loved seeing the shock and worry etched on her face at the library.

Yesterday, he'd just left the mercantile after buying new ammo and happened to see her pass through the intersection. Following with glee, he'd entered the Watering Hole ten minutes after her and grabbed a table in a secluded corner by the restrooms – another stroke of good luck.

But today, he decided he couldn't rely on chance encounters, and his patience in dealing with her was wearing thin since he got a text this morning banning him from Spurs. Another infraction she would pay for, starting tonight.

Getting out of the Jeep, he snuck up to the back door and found the lock as easy to pick as he'd thought. Now, if he managed to avoid the stair creaks in the dark, he could deliver a scare that would ensure Amie's cooperation.

****

A slight noise penetrated Amie's sleep seconds before a heavy weight covered her body and a large hand pressed over her mouth. Sheer black fright swept through her as she struggled to get free in the dark, her heart thundering in her ears. Cal Miller's sinister voice whispered in her ear, and panic like she'd never known before welled in her throat, strangling her breath as effectively as his hand covering her mouth.

"Be still, little girl, and listen."

She ceased moving as anger mingled with trepidation. Never in a million years would she have guessed he would act so brazen as to sneak in here. Then his threat sent a cold chill through her, defusing the heat of her building fury.

"Remember the deer I left for you and your boyfriend? You don't do as I say, I'll make the next gift one of his beloved animals, only I won't kill it first. I do so love to inflict suffering and pain on others." He removed his hand, his breath harsh on her face as he said, "If you scream, I'll hurt whoever barges in here."

Amie gulped in some much-needed air wishing she could see more than his shape hovering above her. She had no doubt he would follow through on those threats, and her heart twisted as she thought of Ben's rescues and what Cal might do to them. And then a sudden thought occurred to her, and she didn't hesitate to ask him about it point-blank.

"You're the sadistic hunter they're searching for, aren't you? The one maiming wildlife and abandoning them to die a slow, horrible death."

His deep chuckle was pure evil and made her skin crawl. "That would be me. It's a fun pastime that helps alleviate the boredom. If you don't want that fate to fall on those llamas or horses or dogs, meet me tomorrow evening. Drive down Highway 6 until you reach a turnoff labeled Pine Tree Road.

Pull onto that road and park then start walking. I'll find you."

"And then what?"

Anyone who could do such things to animals wouldn't hesitate to assist in a suicide or run someone off the road, especially if they perceived them as a threat, leaving no question in her mind he had something to do with Mike's death and was guilty of hurting Myla. She seethed with resentment over the pain he'd caused everyone but wasn't foolish enough to meet him on a deserted road.

"Then I'll set you straight on a few things and you'll leave from there and return to Omaha and stay out of my business from now on."

"And if I don't, you'll hurt Ben's animals?"

"Maybe, or I may get so mad, I'll go after him. Did you know they've banned me from Spurs? That really pisses me off, Amie."

His hard tone sent shivers of unease down her spine, so different from Ben's rigid, commanding voice that she always reacted to with quivers of pleasure. His warning about going after Ben didn't scare her as much. Ben was much smarter than Cal and wouldn't get caught unaware.

"Fine," she bit out, now just wanting him gone. "I'll be there around five o'clock."

Cal rolled off her so fast she wasn't prepared and gasped. When he spoke again, her throat went dry.

"And, Amie? Don't tell *anyone*, or I'll make you sorry. Come alone tomorrow."

The next sound she heard was the door opening then clicking shut. She would grab her gun from the nightstand drawer, but it wouldn't do her a lot of good now. So she went for the next safest thing – her phone.

Her voice shook along with her entire body when Ben answered. "B...Ben? He was here...in m... my room."

Ben swore a blue streak and whipped his vehicle around instead of turning onto his property. A cold knot cramped his gut at the image Amie's scared voice planted in his head. When he got his hands on Miller, he would make him pay for terrorizing her. Thank God she called and didn't try to hide this latest incident from him. Speeding back down the highway toward Mountain Bend, he punched in Drew's number on his cell and relayed what had occurred right under his nose, unable to tone down his worry and anger.

"Jen and I are headed over there now, and I'll

call the sheriff's office to get someone here ASAP."

"Thanks. I'm ten, fifteen minutes tops from your place." He hung up, grateful for friends who understood and acted without questions.

A sheriff's cruiser was already parked out front of Miner's Junction when Ben arrived. He parked behind it and sprinted inside, spotting Amie sitting in the dining room with Jen and Drew. Keith, one of the county deputies, stood with pad and pen in hand, taking notes. Ben took a moment to breathe a sigh of relief at seeing Amie safe and sound before joining them.

Tears filled her eyes as soon as she saw him, tracked down her pale cheeks when he pulled her up, took her chair then settled her on his lap, and she broke into sobs that threatened his control as soon as he wrapped his arms around her.

Drew nodded, concern etched on both his and Jen's faces. "I figured she was holding back," he said, reaching over and squeezing his wife's hand.

Ben's chest constricted at hearing her weep, but he reined in his fury and the urge to rant at someone, anyone, for her sake. Tightening his arms, he glanced up at Keith.

"Did you get enough for now?"

"Sure did. What about your other guests, Drew?

Have you checked on them?"

"Both couples checked out on Monday, which made it easier for this guy to move around upstairs without alerting anyone."

"That and your flimsy locks," Ben retorted.

Keith held up a hand. "No sense in casting blame on anyone except Miller."

Ben sighed, irritated with himself. "You're right, Keith. I'm sorry, Drew."

"Understandable," Drew replied in a regretful voice. "Just because this is a safe town with little crime is no excuse for us to let our guard down."

Closing his notepad, Keith said, "I'll send out an APB..."

"No!" Amie burst out, her body going rigid with the panic he caught in her strident exclamation, her head ramming Ben's chin as she jerked upright. "He warned me about telling anyone." She sat up all the way and looked up at him with a tortured expression. "He swore he'd hurt your animals, or you. He's the hunter you've been searching for all this time and admitted to leaving that deer for us to find."

Ben checked Kevin and Drew's reactions before replying, "I can take care of myself and my livestock, Amie. I promise."

"I know that, but..." She paused, a guilty

expression crossing her face as she added, "there's more involved, more you don't know about him, and me."

"Tell me."

She tried wriggling out of his arms, but he refused to let her escape, wanting to keep her close.

He'd suspected all along she was keeping something from him but never imagined it involved Miller. Her shoulders slumped, and she bit her lower lip, refusing to look at him as she told them about her friends, Mike and Myla, and what they thought Miller had done.

Jesus, she thought to go after a man she is convinced is ruthless enough to run her friend off the road?

"For God's sake, Amie. What were you thinking?" he asked harshly.

"That I would do anything for Myla. You can't understand the bond we share, how close we are." She winced and rushed to correct her error, but he shook his head as painful memories resurfaced.

"No, don't say anything else. Suffice it to say I do understand."

Hadn't he rushed to Bart's rescue numerous times? Wouldn't he have done anything to see his brother safe? Because he could understand her rash thinking, he couldn't judge or get pissed over her reasoning, just over her silence on the matter.

"Why don't we table this discussion until morning, or later this morning?" Keith suggested after checking the time. "I'll fill Shawn in on everything, and he'll take it from there. There's not much else we can do tonight anyway."

"Are you staying the night?" Drew asked Ben.

"Not here. Amie is coming home with me."

"I am?" she asked him, appearing relieved.

Her lack of irritation at his high-handedness spoke volumes. "You are. Ask Shawn to meet me out there, Keith."

"Will do. Take care, everyone."

Keith left as Ben nudged Amie up, Drew and Jen standing along with them. "I'll help Amie get a few things before we leave."

"Take your time. We'll stay here instead of next door for now. I doubt either of us will get any more sleep tonight. Call me if you hear anything," Drew said.

The convenience of living in the house next to their inn had worked in Amie's favor in terms of getting help fast. Ben knew she'd stay safe with the other couple but wasn't about to let her out of his sight until Miller was caught. The guy was more than a sick fuck. He could very well be an attempted murderer.

By the time they reached his place, Amie's eyes were drooping. "Come on," he said, opening his door. "We both need sleep and clearer heads before talking to Shawn tomorrow."

Reaching over with a tentative hand, she said, "I'm sorry for holding back on you and all this trouble."

"Believe it or not after my insistence on open honesty between us, I understand that depth of caring and what drove you to try anything for your friend." After experiencing his volatile reaction when he'd heard her tremulous voice on the phone, he was now sure he loved Amie, a bittersweet revelation given their circumstances. "No reason to apologize again." He squeezed her hand before escorting her inside.

Just like before, she dropped to her knees to greet his dogs. As pleased as he was about her fondness for them, when she stood and asked, "Can Sheba sleep with us?" he wasn't about to allow that.

"Absolutely not. Go to bed, Amie. I'll join you shortly."

"Fine. Sorry, girl," she told the shepherd before picking up her bag and heading toward his room.

Ben woke before Amie, a few hours later, cursing as he struggled to get out of bed around all three dogs. How she managed to let them up without waking him was beyond him, and he would say it was a good thing she was leaving soon before they got used to such luxury, but that wouldn't be true.

He didn't want her to leave but had no say in the matter. The best he could do was ensure her safety both for the remainder of her time here and when she returned to Omaha by helping to put Miller behind bars.

****

Amie roused to men's voices coming from the other room and a soft weight against her legs. She sat up, and Sheba stretched before standing to lick her face. Since Ben was nowhere around, she could only assume he hadn't minded the dogs on the bed.

"I better go see what's going on, since it probably concerns me," she told the shepherd, sliding off the bed.

After using the bathroom and dressing in jeans and a sweatshirt, she padded down the hall, Sheba running ahead of her and straight out to the back dog door as Amie emerged into the living room. Four pairs of eyes zeroed in on her, and heat suffused her face.

Ben glared at Shawn and stated in a hard tone, “No,” then strode toward her and took her hand.

“I’ve filled Shawn, Dakota, and Clayton in on last night and what you told me about Miller.”

“No what?” she asked as he led her to the sofa where Clayton sat on one end. Shawn and Dakota remained standing by the fireplace.

Shawn spoke before Ben. “I mentioned letting you meet Miller today wearing a wire and a tracker. We’d be right there with you, and it would end this faster.”

“Not just no, but hell no,” Ben snapped, trying to pull her down next to him as he took a seat.

Amie tugged out of his grasp and spun toward Shawn. “I agree.” She would do anything to keep Cal from harming anything or anyone else.

“Absolutely not!” Ben jumped to his feet and glared at her. “I won’t even consider it, Amie.”

“You don’t have to,” she retorted. “It’s not up to you, is it, Sheriff?”

“Uh, oh,” Clayton uttered, flicking Ben an amused glance as he crossed one booted foot over his knee.

Shawn glared at Clayton then told Amie, “No, I don’t suppose it is, but...”

"No buts, and shut up, Clayton." Ben sent the prosecutor a scathing glare before rounding on Amie. "It's too dangerous, too much of a risk."

Her heart stuttered at the raw pain reflected in his green eyes, and she realized he was thinking of his brother. She hated putting him in such a position and causing him grief, but she carried her own tortured memories of Mike's death and Myla's suffering, not to mention Cal's threats against Ben and his animals.

"I have to, Ben, for Myla and Mike. Besides, I won't be safe, and neither will you or who knows how many animals, until he's stopped."

"We didn't let that son of a bitch get to Lisa last spring," Dakota grumbled in a rough, hard voice. "You can trust us with your girl."

Clayton stood and faced Ben. "There's safety in numbers, and she has them with all of us, and others when we ask. Once we nab him, I'll take him down the rest of the way." He brushed a hand over Amie's shoulder. "If she's brave enough to try this, you should be proud of her, not stand in her way."

"I want to do it with your blessing and help, but I'll go ahead without either if I must," she told Ben, determined to see an end to Cal's threats.

Ben slid his gaze from her to the three men

offering their protection, his taut shoulders slumping. "You leave me no choice, but nothing better go wrong."

What could go wrong? Amie sat at the table with the men as they went over the details and Shawn explained the wire and tracker, thinking they had everything covered. Now, all she needed to do was get her nausea under control before this evening.

Chapter Eleven

Ben crouched behind the tree, his rifle aimed and cocked for any wrong move once Miller showed his evil face. Watching Amie pull over and get out of her car, her face conveying apprehension and dread, he wanted to rush out and whisk her away from this secluded spot. He never should have agreed to this plan, but her determination and admirable conviction this was the right thing to do left him no choice.

As she ran her trembling hands down her jean-clad thighs and started walking down the dirt road, Ben whispered, "Don't any of you lose sight of her."

"As if," Dakota muttered.

"Be quiet, both of you," Shawn growled. Clayton just chuckled.

"You wouldn't find this amusing, Clayton, if that was Skye out there," Ben said.

"Yeah, you're right, Ben. Sorry," Clayton

replied.

"What part of be quiet don't you understand?" The sheriff's voice rumbled with frustration, and Ben didn't doubt he was imagining Lisa in Amie's position. They all heard the rev of an ATV coming up the road from the opposite direction of where Amie had turned in and stopped. With him and Clayton hidden in the woods on one side of the road and Shawn and Dakota in place among the trees on the other side, she was well covered and protected.

So why was Ben's stomach turning queasy with unease?

"We wait," Shawn reminded them as the all-terrain vehicle roared to a stop in front of Amie who was now way too far away for Ben's peace of mind.

Wearing a motorcycle helmet and camouflage, Miller slid off the sporty three-wheeler and, in a move so fast none of them were prepared, he wrapped an arm around her throat, pulling her back against his front. A knife appeared in his other hand, and he pressed the blade against her throat as he shuffled backward using her as a human shield.

"*Fuck*!" Fury and terror clogged Ben's throat, his finger tightening on the trigger as he stood.

"Move!" Shawn ordered, but Ben was already darting from the woods onto the road.

Clayton, Dakota, and Shawn all emerged from the woods, rifles aimed at the pair, taking slow, measured steps toward them.

"Let her go, you fucking bastard!" Ben shouted.

Miller shook his head, his face hidden behind the helmet's dark visor. He didn't say a word, just pricked Amie's neck enough to draw a bead of crimson blood. She bit her lip, her hair clinging to her perspiration-damp cheeks and neck with the quick negative headshake she gave them. Her bright blue-green eyes didn't reveal fear, remaining steady on him with a confidence he prayed she didn't regret.

"Miller, whatever you're planning, stop and think. We've got you cold." Shawn advanced, moving to the right as Ben and Clayton shuffled forward and left, Dakota taking quiet, menacing steps straight ahead.

Bending his head to Amie's ear, Miller's voice came through the wire into all of their ears. "Tell them to stand down. Then you get on the ATV in front of me without a fight, or I'll slice you from ear to ear."

"I told you this was a mistake," Ben hissed into his mike. Icy fear knotted in his gut as he watched with impotent rage Amie straddling the ATV while Miller kept his stranglehold and the knife against her neck.

"He doesn't know about the wire or tracker," Clayton whispered calmly, lowering his rifle when Miller backed the vehicle into the woods.

"Which works in our favor. Let's go."

Shawn led the way back to his cruiser, and they all piled in, Ben itching to vent his worry and ire on someone, anyone. Before he could, Dakota settled on the rear seat next to him, his dark, granite-hard face filled with understanding.

"He won't hurt her," he vowed, his hard, implacable tone matching the look in his black eyes.

"He's a dead man if he does," Ben promised.

"Agreed."

"You two knock it off." Clayton turned from the front to glare at them. "You can't say shit like that in front of a DA or sheriff, regardless of our friendship."

Dakota shrugged his massive shoulders. "We just did, so deal with it."

If fear for Amie weren't robbing him of all other thought and emotion, Ben would laugh at Clayton's frustration. Instead, he concentrated on listening and plotting as Shawn followed the direction of the green dot from the tracking device in Amie's shoe.

Amie wasn't too worried about how this would

end, just frightened about what Cal might do before the guys rescued her. She hated sitting so close to him, his arms caging her in as he steered the speeding three-wheeler along the narrow, woodsy trail. They bounced so close, some tree branches swiped at her arms and face, snagging her sweatshirt and scratching her skin. Those stings were minor discomforts compared to the knife prick and threat of a deeper cut. She shivered just thinking about that possibility.

Cal's sinister chuckle reverberated in her ear as he said, "I can feel you trembling against me. You're smart to be worried after betraying me."

His threats indicated he wasn't aware of the wire or tracking device the sheriff had outfitted her with. Both offered comfort from worry and fear but didn't completely prevent either emotion from causing her nerves to skitter under her skin. She didn't bother answering him. Between the jarring, uncomfortable ride, the loud motor roaring in her ears, and her skin crawling from Cal's nearness, she couldn't concentrate on anything except Ben coming to her rescue.

After what seemed like hours, the trail ended at a small clearing and an old run-down cabin. Amie's leg muscles quivered as she dismounted the ATV, and Cal gripped her upper arm in a bruising hold.

Yanking her inside, he flung off the helmet and drilled her with a cold-eyed glower. “I didn’t plan to hurt you too much until I saw proof you didn’t heed my warning. Did you and those idiots honestly think I wouldn’t arrive early for such a possibility? I’m good at perching up in a tree and waiting patiently.”

Not knowing how long before the guys arrived, she let him back her against the rough wall and stated with growing confidence, “You ran Myla off the road. Did you also have something to do with Mike’s death?”

“Such topics shouldn’t spew from a pretty mouth.” He backhanded her so fast she nearly crumpled to the floor. Only his tight grip on her arm held her upright as her mouth throbbed, and she tasted blood. “There, not so pretty now,” he sneered. “I didn’t need to help the kid. All I had to do was stand by and watch with a few taunting remarks that ensured he went through with his swan dive. God, that was as much fun to watch as seeing his sister’s car go flying down that ravine. So much better and more satisfying than inflicting pain and suffering on animals.”

Unable to believe he just admitted everything and praying it was all recorded, she whispered,

"You're sick."

"And perverted, don't forget that adjective. I'm particularly fond of that one. Now, what to do with you?"

He released her and strolled across the room toward the bed in the corner. She doubted this run-down shack was the same cabin he'd rented, which made her suspect he had found it for the sole purpose of bringing her here. Thank God she hadn't believed him when he promised all he wanted to do today was talk and send her home.

Amie caught a shadow of movement at the one window a second before the front door went crashing open and the window pane shattered. Cal's shocked, furious expression would have been comical if he hadn't reacted to the four men breaking into the cabin by withdrawing a gun from his waistband.

Pure terror kept her frozen against the wall as he whipped toward her, aimed the gun at her head, and snarled, "Fuck you, bitch!"

The small cabin exploded in gunfire, Ben diving sideways to block Miller's shot if he got one off, firing at Miller along with the others. Cal jerked from the impact of several bullets slamming through his hunting vest and taking him to his knees, arrogant disbelief etched on his stunned face.

"How?" he gasped before toppling sideways, his eyes glassing over in death.

"Too fast and painless," Dakota said, dropping his rifle downward to nudge the body.

"But over and done with," Shawn replied, bending to check for a pulse.

Amie ignored them as Ben picked her up and walked out of the cabin into the cool, darkening mountain air. Brushing his mouth gently over hers, he stated, "I could kill him again for that alone."

She ran her tongue over her throbbing lip. "No need. I'm fine. More than fine if you tell me you all heard his confession."

"Loud and clear, the idiot. For someone who took so many precautions not to get caught, he was too overly confident of you and your compliance. Tell me you're okay," he insisted in a hoarse tone, releasing her legs to slide down to the ground.

Amie loved that concerned, focused look even though she felt bad for worrying him. The shakes were increasing, both inside and out, and she relished the comforting band of his arm around her as she leaned against his strength. "I'm okay now. Sorry for stressing you, but thank you for rescuing me."

"You're welcome. You did what you thought you

should, just don't make a habit of putting yourself in need of rescuing. My heart can't take it."

They both realized at the same time it wouldn't matter since she was leaving soon, and he wouldn't be around to get her out of jams. Ben's jaw went taut, and Amie's heart got that funny clutch whenever she thought of returning home and never seeing him again.

"Do you have to leave right away?" he asked, holding her close.

Pleasure blossomed, easing the quaking of her muscles as Amie thought of all the possibilities of completing her original four-week vacation plans with him. "No, I'm booked at the B&B for another week, and not expected back home until then."

"Spend the week with me, at my place," he offered as the sheriff, Dakota, and Clayton came out of the cabin, Shawn on a radio call.

"Okay." She hurried to agree, not wanting to lose this opportunity amid the chaos of questions and paperwork that was about to ensue over Cal's death.

Shawn ended his conversation and joined them, all three of them eyeing her with intent, dominant concern as the sheriff said, "I have to stick around for a crime scene crew. Ben, why don't you take Amie back, and we can do statements in the morning." He turned to Clayton. "Are you free then to join us?"

"I don't have court tomorrow, so that works. Dakota and I will hang with you here."

Dakota nodded in agreement, both men ignoring Shawn's huff of annoyance. "I don't suppose it would do any good to remind you I'm a big boy and can handle this fine without you?"

"Nope," Dakota returned.

The short exchange spoke volumes about how close the three men were, and when Amie glanced up at Ben, her heart ached at the sadness lurking in his eyes, giving away he was remembering his bond with his brother. Her thoughts jumped to Myla, and she couldn't wait to call her with this news, putting an end to her friend's suffering over Miller not paying for the sins he'd perpetrated against her and Mike.

"If you don't need either of us," Ben stated, "then we'll see you in the morning. I'm assuming you'll have a ride to your cruiser if I take it back to where Amie left her car?"

"No problem. We have to get the ATV and Miller's Jeep returned also. Amie, take care." Shawn ran a hand down her hair, tears pricking her eyes at the comforting gesture.

"Thank you, all of...you." She choked up but managed to add, "I'm sorry for the trouble I've caused."

All four men frowned, but it was Ben who answered. "I'm still working on getting her to stop apologizing all the time when it's not necessary."

Clayton gave her a teasing grin but addressed Ben. "Work harder."

Despite the last harrowing hours, Amie went with Ben with a light step and surge of warmth dispelling the last of the coldness dealing with Cal had instilled in her. The only thing dampening her excitement for spending the upcoming days with him was her inevitable leave-taking. She would not only miss her Dom but her new friends, and the small town she'd grown to like so much.

****

Ben groaned above Amie's straining body, driving into her clasping pussy two more times before slowing and pulling out of her slick pussy, lowering her legs from his shoulders on his way. Keeping her pinned to his bed with his body was fast becoming his favorite pastime, and the only way he could keep from replaying that scene in the woods when Miller had turned his gun on her. His first thought in those few seconds of mind-numbing terror was *not again*; he couldn't act too late again to save someone he loved.

The sheer fright on her face, along with her bleeding, bruised mouth, had fueled his rage past his concern, and he couldn't have asked for a more satisfying outcome once he got himself under control. Admitting the depth of his feelings and coming so close to losing her in the same breath had shaken him as forcefully as losing his twin. He owed his friends an apology now that he knew how easy it was to fall fast and hard for the right woman.

Amie moaned as she straightened her legs, and, despite the flush of pleasure staining her cheeks and the sated glaze in her bright eyes, he could still detect the strain of the last few days on her face. Listening to her cry as she'd spoken to her friend last night and then watching her struggle through giving her statement the next morning in Shawn's office had forced him to rein in the urge to whisk her away from everyone. He hadn't liked holding back, watching her suffer, but understood the necessity. What was between her and Myla was personal, and between her and Shawn, a legal issue he couldn't interfere with.

"I may never walk again," she murmured in

drowsy contentment.

"Yes, you will. Did you enjoy visiting with the girls tonight, or was it too stressful?"

They'd stayed home from the club last night, Ben thinking she needed to rest and recuperate from the previous twenty-four hours. Because of a meeting about their fundraiser next weekend, he'd caved and taken her over to Shawn's place, leaving her with the girls while the Masters finalized their plans.

"They were wonderful, supportive, and nonjudgmental, which I appreciate. At least no one except you has mentioned I should have come clean about my reason for vacationing here a lot sooner." She frowned, glaring at him.

Ben tweaked a nipple, loving the way she didn't hesitate to call him on his overprotectiveness, but reminding her when and where he would not tolerate such looks. "Remember where you are," he warned her. "At least for this next week." Mentioning her departure next Sunday was more for him than her.

She rubbed her still-damp body against his. "I'm not likely to forget that, only so many rules."

"Then I'll have fun reminding you. Go to sleep. If it warms up tomorrow, we can go for a short ride after we finish work."

Throwing her arms around his neck, she squeezed, the spontaneous hug of delight almost as satisfying as climaxing inside her snug body.

"Okay."

The week passed way too fast for Ben, and with each day, he grew more accustomed to having Amie around, sharing his space and his bed. The more he was around her, the more he found to like. She pitched in around the house without him asking, and he doubted the place had ever been so clean. He arrived home on Tuesday to find her helping Joaquin muck out the stalls, straw in her hair, dirt smudged on her face, and a beaming smile his hired hand was eating up. On Wednesday, he took off early and drove her into Boise for dinner at his favorite steak house. When she excused herself to use the restroom and took that opportunity to ask the kitchen for bones for the dogs, he'd delayed her orgasm until she apologized for going behind his back to spoil them even though he didn't mind them having the bones. He did take exception to them on the bed but still woke every morning fighting his way around all three, the tormented frustration he'd put Amie through failing to stop her from sneaking the dogs up on the bed after he fell asleep.

"Do you want to go to the club tonight or stay

home?" he asked her as they finished dinner. "I have to give you a heads-up about tomorrow night's fundraiser. Since you're so new to everything yet, you might find some of the games too intense for your comfort. We can go tonight and play, which will give you more public experience before you leave Sunday in case you decide to sit out tomorrow."

Whenever he found himself wishing she would stay, he made a point of mentioning her upcoming departure, hoping she would show a willingness to keep their relationship going. Other than the fleeting shadows of sadness in her eyes, she didn't reveal her thoughts on the subject, and he didn't want to push.

Ben figured she was going over all her options. Thinking of some of the games he would love to participate in with her, he injected a note of authority in his tone to prompt her to open up. "What are you thinking, Amie? Maybe I can help."

"I suppose this is one of those times you want complete transparency."

"You suppose correctly. You don't have to participate in the games to attend tomorrow if that's what're thinking."

"I'll stay with you, right? I don't want to be pawned off on someone else during a game."

"I don't share, in case you haven't caught on

to that by now." Ben stood and gathered up their plates. At least she wasn't contemplating expanding her experience to include other Doms while here. It was hard enough to keep his emotions in check whenever he thought of her attending a club in Omaha.

"Okay, then I wish to stay here tonight and go to Spurs tomorrow. It sounds like fun." Her eyes shifted over to the windows where he had made good on one of the suggestions he'd mentioned last week for getting creative.

He could see her pulse jump in her neck thinking about how he'd bound her wrists to her ankles and fucked her from behind in front of the floor-to-ceiling glass panes. She cut her gaze toward him, a blush stealing over her face.

"I like what you do here as much as at Spurs, maybe more so because I'm not self-conscious about other people." A teasing glint lit up her eyes. "And I want you all to myself one more night."

"You could have me to yourself every night if you would consider relocating," he returned, tossing the suggestion out there to get her reaction.

Amie's eyes widened and filled with longing before regret chased away that brief revelation. "As tempting as that is, I can't imagine living anywhere else. Omaha is home, where my best friend is and where I'm comfortable."

He could read her like a book by now, and was sure something else went through her head just then, but Ben didn't pursue the matter. He opened the door, leaving the next step, if there was one, up to Amie.

"I can understand that as I wouldn't want to leave my place here, or the life I've made for myself." He loaded the plates in the dishwasher then turned to her as she joined him at the sink, pinning her against the counter with his body. "But we have thirty-six hours before you leave. Let's see how creative I can get tonight and how daring I can tempt you to be tomorrow."

Chapter Twelve

Ben dared her to wear nothing except his shirt to Spurs the following night. Amie accepted because she would do anything to please him at this point. She was desperate to ensure she left him with memories he wouldn't forget anytime soon and to leave tomorrow with those same memories permanently etched into her brain. She didn't want to forget anything about him or this trip, not even Cal Miller. If it hadn't been for him, she never would have met her Dom cowboy.

Hugging her sweater coat around her, she glanced at his rugged profile in the dark SUV as he turned off the main highway onto the narrow two-lane road leading to Spurs. Her heart flip-flopped, and her throat went dry and tight, the same as when he'd suggested she could move out here with him. She wanted to, at least long enough to see if their feelings involved more than mutual attraction and an infatuation with her first Dom.

He was everything she'd always wanted in a man and then some. She'd even fallen head over heels for his sexual dominance, but since she'd caved so fast to a man's control after years of walking away from overbearing men, how did she know she wasn't just fixating on the first man who had read her correctly and proceeded to give her what she'd never realized she needed? Okay, the odds were slim that was the case – there was too much else to like about him for her to limit her feelings to lust.

She would never forget the way he and the others had come to her rescue or her fear for Ben when he'd risked his life by throwing himself in front of her when Cal turned his gun on her. Even getting kidnapped and threatened by that lunatic hadn't scared her as much as Ben's heroic move.

But like and gratitude weren't love, and change didn't come easy for her. She had to be sure before she gave up everything for a man for the first time. Tonight, she planned to push out of her comfort zone and join the activities since she already knew she wouldn't continue exploring with anyone else once she returned to Omaha.

A high-pitched squeal echoed from the side of the building as Ben took her hand and led her toward the entrance. Charlotte, a member Amie had met only once, came dashing around the corner. The lights shone on her oil-slicked nakedness as she paused, breathing heavy, excitement written all over her face.

"Did you see...*eeek*!" She took off again, Nick and Simon hot on her heels as they chased her around to the other side.

"It looks like those three have started their own takedown game," Ben said, holding open the door.

"Takedown?" A stab of envy pierced Amie when she witnessed the fun Charlotte was having and how comfortable she appeared running around naked with two men chasing her.

Placing a hand on her lower back, he ushered her inside before answering. "Subs are oiled up and given a head start before their Dom goes in search of her." His eyes sparked with humor when he added, "They run faster when it's cooler outside."

"Or slower so they can get warmed up another way?"

"Possibly, but that would end the fun too fast. I'll hang up your wrap."

When he eyed his khaki T-shirt with the park rangers' logo and her bare legs, he nailed her in place with a searing look that dispelled the goose bumps from the cooler air. Pulling her against him, he ran a hand up her thigh, hiking up the shirt until he cupped one buttock.

"I'll have to remember to challenge you again tonight. I like the results."

Amie loved that gruff tone as much as his calloused palm scratching her skin. "Okay," she answered, willing to agree to just about anything to reap as many rewards and memories from tonight as possible.

The first people she noticed upon entering the club playroom were the three men standing at the bar conversing with Shawn and Clayton. Tall and dark didn't begin to do them justice, and even though she possessed no desire for anyone other than Ben right now, that didn't prevent a slow curl of lust in her lower abdomen. There was something primal about the men who looked enough alike they were obviously related, a wildness that would dampen any sane woman's panties.

"Are you going to tell me what's running through your head as you ogle our hosts for tonight?" Ben drawled.

Huffing a short laugh, she shook her head. "No way."

Before either of them could say anything else,

Skye rushed up to Amie and threw her arms around her. "I'm so glad you're all right and so sorry you went through such a terrifying ordeal."

"Thanks, Skye." Amie was as touched by her embrace as she was when each of them had called to check on her and offer support.

Releasing her, Skye asked Ben, "Sir, do you mind if Amie sits with us until the games start?"

"No, go ahead. I'll come get you shortly, Amie."

He brushed his hand over her butt then walked toward the bar and joined the three men Amie didn't know. "Who are they?" she asked Skye.

"The McCullough brothers. Clayton introduced me earlier. The one in the middle is Cody and it's his wife, Olivia, who works with the women's shelters. Hot, aren't they?"

"God, yes. I'm glad I'm not the only one drooling despite having my own man candy tonight."

Skye laughed. "I hear you."

Amie was bombarded with questions and concerned inquiries as soon as she sat down at the table with Lisa, Poppy, and Skye. After thanking them and assuring everyone she wasn't suffering any side effects from the ordeal, she picked up one of the papers lying on the table and read the first thing on a list.

"What's this? Bobbing for ducks? Fifty dollars?"

"A list of the games and entry costs," Lisa answered. "Don't worry, the guys pay the fees. All we have to do is volunteer as guinea pigs for their sadistic games."

Poppy laughed. "Don't let her fool you, Amie. We're all looking forward to some of those."

"I'm looking forward to all of them," Kathie said, taking a seat, picking up a sheet, and eyeing the list with a grin. "Especially the auction."

"Auction? The bobbing for ducks and rope tying sound intriguing, but an auction means going off with the highest bidder, right?" That didn't appeal to her at all.

"Yes, but our guys, which I'll bet includes Ben, won't sign up for that one. From what Shawn told me, mostly unattached Doms and subs and those couples who like to invite a third to join them participate." Lisa's gaze shifted over Amie's shoulder and lit up. "Speaking of Master Shawn, I think we're about to begin."

A bell clanged, and the room grew quiet as everyone focused on Master Shawn. There were a lot more people tonight than the other times Amie had visited, and she guessed some were infrequent members who had come tonight to support a good cause and their friends.

"All of the games will commence in a few minutes, each one running for an hour before a winner is declared and a new game begins. Prizes will be handed out at the end of the evening. Check your times for each game you're signed up for and have fun."

Amie's self-consciousness over wearing nothing except Ben's shirt went up another notch as she watched him come toward her with a predatory gleam in his eyes.

"Oh, girlfriend, you are going to have so much fun." Poppy leaned over and whispered to her. "Almost as much fun as me."

Amie noticed Dakota right behind Ben, the big Dom's look as intent and scorching as Ben's, but she shook her head. "Nope. Maybe the same amount, but not less." Not with the way she went hot and wet without a thought to where she was.

Ben held out his hand, and she clasped it, a surge of lust-induced adrenaline pumping through her veins as he pulled her to her feet.

"We're in the first round of rope bondage. The snugness of the rope can cause panic the first time, but I'll be right there, and I'm fast. The winner is whoever finishes first, and, given the speed with which I'll bind then release you, I figure it is a good time to introduce you to something new."

The only thing on Amie's mind when they joined four other couples was the need to not disappoint Ben tonight. As the Masters undressed their subs, she recalled the thrill she experienced when Master Nick had viewed her bare body. Her breath quickened as she looked up at Ben and encountered his patient, calm expression waiting for her agreement.

"I'm counting on you to win this one," she said then pulled the shirt over her head.

"When have I let you down?"

Never. Even knowing she was keeping something from him, he'd never wavered in what he labeled his Dom duty in looking out for her best interests.

"You haven't. You're the best Dom I've ever had," she told him with a cheeky grin.

He didn't rise to the bait and remind her he was her only Dom thus far, instead guiding her to stand in a taped off square a few feet from the woman next to her and turned to the man approaching them. She found it easier to stand there naked with so many people wandering around when she wasn't the only one but still flushed under the appreciative eye of one of the McCulloughs.

"I'm Master Gavin and the judge for this game." He rested a possessive hand on the lower back of the pregnant woman at his side. "This is my wife, Aislyn. Thank you for coming tonight, and good luck."

Before she could respond, he moved on to the next couple, and her attention switched to watching Ben unwind a length of rope from the coil he held in his other hand. Such a simple action, yet sexy as hell, and she suddenly couldn't wait to feel the rope tightening around her because that meant he would have his hands on her again.

"Gavin is introducing himself to the last participants then he'll say start and set a timer. Remember, feel free to use the safewords at any time. Don't hold back for the sake of the game if you're on the verge of panic, Amie, or you'll earn your first public punishment."

She nodded, heeding the warning in his tone but not concerned. Given the rapid rise of her arousal already, she wouldn't need anything except Ben tonight, not if this was the end of her time with him.

"Hands behind your back," Ben instructed as soon as Gavin started the game.

True to his word, he moved swiftly, roping her arms together from wrists to elbows, the snug compression forcing her shoulders back, which pushed her chest forward. She bit her lip as he looped the rope around each breast, leaving her nipples jutting out and going numb before crisscrossing the end over her waist, hips, and upper thighs. Her already shallow breathing snagged when he drew the rough hemp up between her labia next, the coarse fibers abrading her clit as he tugged upward then secured the end at her waist. His focused attention on her face helped her remain calm as she tested her confinement. Her body quaked from her inability to move, but she managed to concentrate on Ben without panicking.

"Done!" Ben called out without taking his eyes off her.

"You're as fast as I remember from a few years ago. Congratulations." Master Gavin winked at Amie before announcing the second and third-place winners.

"Thanks," Ben said before bending to whisper to Amie, "I'm so fucking proud of you." He brushed his thumbs over her nipples then started to uncoil the rope.

Basking in his praise, she was almost sorry when he released her even though she could breathe easier. Then needle pinpricks of pain stabbed at her nipples with the return of blood flow, and she slapped her freed hands over the throbbing tips with a scowl.

"You could have warned me," she muttered, conscious of the people near enough to hear.

Picking up his shirt, Ben dropped it over her head, ignored her complaint, and grabbed her hand. "Let's check out the buffet before our next game."

Amie couldn't stay annoyed, not when her nipples started throbbing, her tender clit ached for more attention, and her stomach rumbled when she saw the array of catered appetizers.

"Okay, I forgive you," she said when he handed her a plate.

"I figured you would. I experimented with nipple clamps before applying them to a sub for the first time and remember what happened when I released them." He flicked a glance at her breasts and her nipples' noticeable pucker under the shirt. "I remember what came after the discomfort."

The fact he would put himself through that before subjecting someone else to it was one more thing to admire and like about her Dom cowboy, and Amie realized her departure tomorrow was getting harder and harder to think about. To take her mind off it, she eyed the fancy spread, wanting to try one of everything.

"Everything looks so good," she said, selecting two spinach-and-feta-filled Phyllo pastries.

"Try these. Smoked Danish bacon with a bourbon glaze. They're my favorite." Ben placed three of the skewered treats on her plate.

"I wasn't that hungry until now."

An auburn-haired woman with friendly gray eyes came up next to her, one hand going to her rounded belly, the other holding a full plate. "Me either, but this guy is always hungry. I'm Olivia McCullough."

"Nice to meet you. I'm Amie, and Ben, um, Master Ben," she amended when he nudged her, "mentioned you and your work with women's shelters. I'm glad I was here to contribute tonight."

"I appreciate your support. It's nice of the new owners to continue with Master Randy's fundraiser."

"Nice or diabolical?" Amie asked when the sub auction was announced.

Olivia laughed. "Maybe both."

"I met your sister-in-law. It's nice you'll have babies close to the same time."

"Which one? Roz and Aislyn are both pregnant, but Roz took longer so she's due a few months after us."

"We planned it that way. I'm Cody, Olivia's husband." Cody placed his hand over Olivia's on her stomach, his blue eyes twinkling.

Ben snorted. "I believe it. As close as the three of you are, I wouldn't be surprised if you were in the same room."

"If you're envious, Wilcox, you can always join the ranks of wedded bliss."

Amie felt Ben stiffen next to her and wondered if Cody's remark made him think of her or his brother and decided she didn't want to know.

"Maybe someday," he replied, taking her elbow. "If you'll excuse us, we'll catch you later."

Cody nodded, and Olivia said, "Nice to meet you, Amie."

"Same here." As Ben led her to a table, she tried to defuse the awkward silence between them. "They're nice. What did you sign us up for next?"

"Yeah, they are." They joined Dakota who held Poppy on his lap and was feeding her the last bite of a mini taco, before he answered, "Bobbing for ducks, but not for another thirty minutes."

"That sounds like fun. Are we in that one?" Poppy asked Dakota.

"We can be, if you want to."

Amie stabbed a meatball. "Rubber ducks have

to be easier than apples," she said, thinking of the one time she'd tried bobbing for apples at a party.

"We'll see if you think so shortly," was all the explanation Ben offered.

"Now I definitely want in," Poppy asserted.

Amie wasn't as sure as Poppy, and when she read the waterproof ink on some of the bath toys lined up along the hot tub's ledge, she became even less sure. Acts such as licking, biting, and sucking were written on the yellow ducks while the blue ones were labeled with body parts.

"Non-slip mats have been added to the spa to ensure safety. Each sub bobs for one yellow and one blue duck at a time with hands tied behind her back," Clayton announced.

Five others besides herself were waiting next to their Doms to participate, and several onlookers were lounging around, waiting for the entertainment. The cool night air did little to reduce the heat crawling up Amie's neck and face as she imagined performing a blowjob or any of the other sexual combos in front of others. She shuffled closer to Ben, intending to ask him about backing out, but glimpsing the tender expression on his face as he leaned down muddled her thinking long enough for him to speak first.

"Would you rather watch?"

No, not if it means disappointing you or missing out on another awesome memory to remember you by. Amie's misgivings fled, and excitement grabbed hold. Shaking her head, she reached for the hem of his shirt and pulled it up.

"No. Let's win another."

With a hand on her bare butt, he replied, "This one is up to you."

Amie handed him the shirt as he took a pair of cuffs from Clayton. "Two minutes," Clayton warned then tossed another pair to Dakota.

Watching Ben strip, her pulse went haywire. Licking her lips, she went over the rules again so she didn't screw up. "You'll sit on the seat while I get a duck in each color then return to you and do what's written, right?"

"Correct." He discarded his jeans on a bench and grabbed her hand, winking as she eyed his erection. "Keep looking at me like that, and we will skip this. Remember, the winning team is the one who does the most ducks, so to speak."

"Got it. A lot of work for me, and a lot of fun for you."

"Now you're catching on."

****

With five large men seated in the hot tub and five subs splashing around between them, the spa was crowded with naked bodies. Ben didn't care for shedding all his clothes in front of so many, but watching Amie get into the swing of the game was worth any price. He thought she'd done well with the rope tying considering that was her first time experiencing public exposure, but it only took bobbing for her first two ducks then following the notes for her to shed the rest of her inhibitions.

"Kiss and lips," she read, standing between his spread thighs as he held the rubber toys. Eyes sparkling, she leaned forward.

Since her hands were cuffed, he helped her keep her balance by cupping her face, his hold secure as she moved those soft lips over his. When she lingered too long, he pushed her up with a reminder.

"On to the next ones, and hurry. You're behind." A quick scan around the hot tub showed the other girls were already returning for the second round.

Amie spun around, giggling when she almost lost her balance, then hurried to dive for the closest floating duck. Like before, she dropped it in his hand and retrieved the opposite color.

"Lick nipples," he read for her to speed things up, his cock jerking as she ran her tongue over his left then right nipple. When she made to return to the left, he gripped her upper arms, pulled her closer so he could reciprocate with a taste of her turgid nubs, and then turned her with a swat that bounced her buttock.

"Next."

This time the others were all still bobbing, and Ben noticed the other Doms were enjoying their laughing and splashing as much as he. Amie was third to bring back both ducks, and when he held them up so she could read them, her face suffused with color and her breathing quickened. She was such a delightful open book.

"Caress cock. I'll need my hands."

The breathless catch in Amie's voice coupled with the lust stamped on her face sent Ben's blood pumping faster. Reaching behind her, he released her hands then lifted out of the water to sit on the edge with his feet on the spa's bench.

Sinking to her knees between his legs, she wrapped both warm, wet hands around his jutting cock, her light grip enough to ignite an arc of electric heat from base to cock head. To keep from reaching for her and taking control, he leaned back on his fisted hands.

"I...I'm not very good at this," she whispered,

tightening her fingers then stroking up and down his throbbing length.

"Could have fooled me," he rasped, biting back a curse when she brushed a thumb over his seeping slit.

Pleasure lit up her face. "Really?" She looked back down, bit her lower lip, and surprised him when she lowered her head to take him in her mouth.

Fuck. He wasn't prepared for the fiery heat of her lips and tongue. In the past week, he'd fucked her in every position possible, but fellatio was one act they hadn't gotten around to because he was always too eager to get inside her.

"Amie, that's not what you're supposed to do." But, God help him, he didn't want her to stop.

Instead of answering, she held tighter at the base while dragging her lips up his rigid length, her tongue in constant motion circling, licking, stroking. Giving up, he gripped her head, eased her down again, and gritted his teeth as she hollowed her cheeks and sucked hard.

"Son of a bitch, babe, I thought you weren't good at this. It's not nice to lie to your Dom." Amie's chuckle reverberated around his shaft, her hard nipples grazing his thighs from her bent position. They already forfeited the game – not that he cared

– and Ben's need for her had surpassed the point of waiting. "Enough," he demanded as she reached under him to roll his balls in her palm.

He drew her head up, not expecting her to snap at him. "Damn it, why'd you stop me? I wanted..."

"I know what you wanted, but not here, not now. Later."

Ben hauled her out as he stood then signaled Clayton. "We're bowing out."

A knowing smirk played around Clayton's lips. "I already figured. Catch you later."

"Thanks." Turning to Amie, he stated, "Unless you want me to haul you through the room and upstairs naked, put my shirt back on."

After working his damp legs into his jeans, he wasn't about to struggle with zipping over his throbbing erection. Amie was still tugging the shirt down when he hoisted her over his shoulder and strode inside with one hand on her ass. Other than a loud sigh, she kept quiet until he reached a vacant room, and, not bothering to shut the door, dumped her on the bed.

"You...you could have given me time..."

"No, I couldn't," he interrupted her, shucking out of his jeans again then coming down on top of her. "And it's your fault I couldn't wait."

Ben surged inside her slick depths, loving the way her legs and arms wrapped around him and held tight for the wild ride she knew was coming and embraced. The fact he couldn't seem to get enough of her was one more indication she was the one for him, but she'd remained silent when he'd suggested she could stay with him, and he wouldn't mar their final hours together by pleading or arguing for something she didn't want.

"Ben, *yes*," she gasped in his ear, her breath warm, her plea needy as she arched against his pounding hips.

"Now, Amie."

One more time to fuck her, to hold her through the night, to hear her say she was sorry when she shouldn't, not if Omaha was home and where she needed to be.

Chapter Thirteen

"Finally!" Myla squealed as soon as she opened the door.

With a laugh, Amie threw herself into her best friend's arms, surprised at how good Myla looked. "I'm glad to be home."

That wasn't entirely true, she admitted, stepping back and spotting Matt sitting in the living room. Disappointment swamped her even though she was happy they were now a couple. His presence dashed her hope for some private girl talk. She really needed Myla's input on her confused feelings since leaving Mountain Bend fifty-two hours ago.

The farther she'd driven away from Ben and her new friends, the heavier her heart had pressed against her chest. After arriving late last night, exhausted and needing sleep, she'd spent the first night home in her own bed tossing and turning, missing Ben's large body curled around her, the weight of the dogs against her legs, and his grumbling about them on the bed that morning when she arose. Instead of excited about seeing Myla again while driving over here, all she could think about were the vast differences between the small town of Mountain Bend and Omaha's teeming metropolis. In the last four weeks, she hadn't missed fighting big city traffic.

"You're a better influence on her than me," Amie told Matt, padding over to give him a hug.

"Hey! Give me a little credit, will ya?" Myla threw herself onto the couch with a mock glare. "I am the one who did all the therapy, and believe me, it wasn't easy."

"And she was quite vocal about the strain on her." Matt bent and gave her pouting mouth a lingering kiss.

Amie couldn't believe the stab of jealousy poking her over that kiss and forced it away the best she could. She would never begrudge Myla her happiness.

"Okay you." Myla shoved him away with a laugh. "Go away so we can talk. Amie has a lot of gaps to fill in that have nothing to do with that scumbag Miller."

Myla always understands. Amie should have

remembered that.

"Got it. I'll return with lunch in a few hours." He embraced Amie again, whispering in her ear, "Thank you. That must have been a traumatic ordeal for you, and I'll never forget the risk you took to free her."

Amie's throat clogged with tears as she choked, "I had a lot of help that I couldn't have survived without."

"Knock off the whispering, you two. Scram, Matt."

"Going, Myla," he returned, chuckling.

As soon as the door closed behind him, Myla drew her over to Amie's favorite chair. "Sit, talk. What haven't you told me?"

Settling on the recliner, Amie gave her a rueful look. "I won't bother asking what makes you think I left anything out of my calls."

Myla always knew when she was keeping something from her, and she didn't bother anymore. From their first meeting, Ben, too, had read her as well as her best friend. That alone should have told her he was different from the men who had come and gone in her life. Before getting into that, she insisted on hearing what the Omaha police said about Cal's taped confession Shawn shared with them.

"First, did the cops close your case or find out anything more about Cal Miller?"

"Yes, my case is closed, thanks to your bravery. A background check revealed he was an only child and had inherited a butt load of money when his parents died. School records recorded numerous incidents of bullying, but as an adult, he was good at hiding his sadistic side. Now, tell me more about your heroic rescue from the creep. I swear my heart went green with envy when you mentioned those four guys. Tell me they are as hot as you made them sound."

Amie pictured all four, but it was Ben's face that popped up first and stayed in the forefront. "With a capital H, all of them Doms at their club. You were right, by the way. Spanking can be a lot of fun."

Myla burst out laughing. "Told ya! Something tells me you didn't play the field while visiting that club though."

How could she consider anyone else after Ben?

"Uh, oh. You fell for him, didn't you? Your Ben." Myla's tone held a hint of accusation, her face reflecting concern.

"Yes. No. Shit, I don't know." But she did. That was the only thing that explained her mixed emotions. "Myla, my life is here, *you're* here. And long-distance relationships never work."

Myla blew out a breath, gazing at her with compassion. "I didn't say I don't understand. Only you can decide what or who you want, and if he's worth the change in your life." She shook a finger at her. "But don't you dare use me as an excuse, girlfriend. I don't want you to live so far away. I also don't want you to lose someone special because of me. Thanks to you, I have Matt, and I would never begrudge you the same happiness."

"I just got back. I'll give it time. It's too big of a decision to jump into. In the meantime, Matt appeared at home here."

Regret flashed in Myla's eyes. "I made him work for it, that's for sure. He put up with a lot of crap from me and yet, still came back. When I got to where I craved having him around more than I resented my helplessness, I took your advice and gave him a chance."

"I'm glad. It's obvious he's crazy about you and wants to be here."

You could have me to yourself every night if you would consider relocating.

Amie still recalled the immediate thrill that swept through her when Ben tossed that out, and the way his green eyes had bored into her with a burning hunger that went beyond lust. She'd experienced the same yearning until she went cold at the thought of the change taking him up on that offer would entail.

Myla regarded her with a small smile. "Yeah, he is, and does. I'm as sure of that as I am your Ben is just as special, and that's all I'm saying on the subject. The rest is up to you as long as you don't use me as an excuse because you're afraid of change."

Is that what I'm doing? She asked herself that over and over while trying to settle back into her usual routine during the next week. Even though there was pleasure in the familiar, such as Sunday dinner with her parents, wine and popcorn movie night with Myla, and reconnecting with friends in her apartment complex, she failed to achieve the contentment of her life before taking off for Idaho.

Working from home held less appeal without the view of snow-capped mountains from her window or a dog lying next to her chair. Other than their standing Thursday night get-together, Myla was with Matt, and Amie didn't wish to intrude on their time. She picked up food at her favorite restaurants, yet no one greeted her by name.

And she missed Ben every waking moment, dreamed about him every night, yearned for him with every breath. Friday night, she went clubbing with several people, compared every man to Ben, and found them lacking. None focused on her, and only her, while talking or dancing. They gazed at her with lust but without the blood-pumping heat in Ben's eyes. Their voices didn't compel her to open up, didn't censure for her evasiveness, and didn't turn her knees rubbery issuing dominant commands.

The second week, Amie added two new accounts to her already busy workload, hoping the extra hours would help her sleep at night and give her less time to fret. By the weekend, she'd finally readjusted to her regular routine and managed a decent night's sleep.

Then Ben called.

Other than her text to him when she arrived back in Omaha, they hadn't communicated. Seeing his number when she picked up her buzzing phone caused her pulse to flutter. Her heart executed a familiar slow roll upon hearing his deep baritone resonate in her ear when she answered, and she went damp at his simple greeting.

"Hello, Amie. How are you?"

God, she'd missed him. "I'm fine." Could he hear the lie as well as he used to see it on her face? "How about you?"

"Other than being unable to find someone at

Spurs to torment, trying to keep the dogs off the bed, and people asking me if I've heard from you, I'm fine. Now, you try replying with as much honesty."

She couldn't help but smile at his gruff, commanding tone, and the pleasure she reaped from his roundabout way of confessing he missed her. "Other than unable to find someone I want to go out with, putting up with Myla's nagging, and missing the dogs, I'm fine."

"Do you miss me, Amie?"

"Yes, I do," she returned without hesitation. "But..."

"Yeah, I know, that doesn't change anything. If it ever does, you know where to find me. Take care, Amie."

He hung up without giving her a chance to answer, and she went to bed missing him more than ever.

"You're a fucking idiot." Myla pushed past Amie into her apartment and whirled on her with hands fisted on her hips. "And you look awful."

"I love you, too," Amie said coolly, irritated with her for pointing out what she already knew. "Is that why you've dropped in, to put me down?"

"Oh, knock it off and quit playing the martyr. I've watched you pine for that man for two weeks, using me, your parents, and a bunch of other lame excuses for not going back. When you turned down another invitation to go out with me and Matt, I decided to quit babying you. Answer me one question."

"Do I have a choice?" Shutting the door, Amie tried to stifle her irritation as she stalked into the kitchen. It was true she preferred staying home to being a third wheel when Myla went out with Matt. What was so wrong with that? "Wine?"

"It's ten a.m."

"As good a time as any. What's your question?" She opened the refrigerator and grabbed the bottle.

"Do you love him?"

Leaning her forehead against the refrigerator, Amie tried calming her rapid breathing. *I am a coward*, she thought, afraid to admit why her feelings scared her.

"Amie." Myla laid a hand on her shoulder, and she turned to face the person who knew her best, the person she would do anything for, the one she didn't want to betray. "And there it is, the truth. You don't want to hurt me. Girlfriend, what am I going to do with you?"

"What are you talking about?" She shoved by her and got down two glasses.

"Do you honestly think I'd stand in the way

of you and a special relationship?" Myla sighed in exasperation. "Amie, our friendship isn't based on location. You are my closest friend, and that will never change no matter where we live."

Was she right? Would their friendship endure over the long haul of living so far apart? And why hadn't she realized that worry was the crux of her indecision?

"Answer me, Amie. Do you love him?"

She thrust a glass of wine at her. "Yes, I do," she replied then downed her drink.

"Then I'm as happy for you as you are for me. Now, let's get you packed up. That man won't wait forever."

Stunned, nervous, and excited, Amie followed Myla to her bedroom, stuttering, "J-just like that? Pack up and arrive on his doorstep?"

"Unless you have a better way of getting there with all your stuff. Grab your suitcases." Myla started tossing her clothes on the bed, her enthusiasm and optimism contagious.

She remembered Ben saying last night if she changed her mind, she knew where to find him. That was as close to an invitation as she was going to get, and she decided to take it, and him.

"If this doesn't work out, I'm coming back to

kick your butt."

Myla snorted, dumping her underwear drawer into a suitcase. "You and what army? Get a move on. I don't want you driving after dark."

"Yes, Mom."

With a giggle, she tossed a pair of panties at her. "You were honestly afraid we'd lose this because of a few miles between us?"

"Can I help it if he's the first man to muddle my thinking?" she admitted, throwing the panties back at her.

"That should have been your first clue there would be no going back."

Amie pulled in front of Ben's house Sunday afternoon after driving over ten hours the day before, her nerves taut as a bowstring, her heart lodged somewhere in her throat. Myla was right; there was no going back this time, not unless he booted her out. A truck was also in his drive, and, as she got out, she heard voices coming from behind the house. Disappointed he wasn't alone, she walked around back, halting when she spotted Ben astride a stunning, bucking horse. Brown with white mane and tail, the mare appeared unhappy with having someone riding her.

Dakota leaned on the fence rail, keeping watch,

and she managed to remain unnoticed until the dogs saw her and came bounding over. Even though she couldn't take her eyes off Ben's masterful control in staying on the thrashing horse, she couldn't resist dropping to her knees and hugging the dogs.

"I missed you, too," she crooned, laughing as they mauled her with their tongues and bodies. "Okay, enough."

She got to her feet just as Ben managed to bring the horse to heel. With a snort and head toss, the horse still appeared skittish but seemed willing to walk around carrying her rider without attempting to dislodge him. With slow steps so as not to distract Ben, she joined Dakota at the rail. He surprised her when he turned, thumbed his Stetson up enough for her to see the sardonic lift of one black brow, and greeted her with drawled humor that matched the twinkle in his midnight eyes.

"'Bout time you got your ass back here, girl."

Before she could form a reply to that unexpected statement, Ben dismounted and swung his gaze toward them. Her throat went dry as she eyed the vee of his exposed, sweat-damped chest from his unbuttoned black shirt, the brown suede vest, leather gloves, and chaps framing his pelvis adding to his rugged, lust-inducing appearance. But it was the look of heated possessiveness lighting up his razor-sharp green eyes that weakened her knees and stole her breath.

"I think that's my cue to hightail it out of here." Dakota lifted a hand to Ben. "She's all yours. Let me know if you have any trouble with her."

He pivoted and walked away, leaving her alone with Ben as he swooped down to pick up his hat, slapped it on, and stalked toward her with purpose etched on his tanned face. The only thing she could think of to say when he stopped in front of her with nothing but the wooden fence separating her from his glistening, towering body was, "Aren't you cold?"

"No." Ben swung over the fence, gripped her arm, and hauled her against him. "It's about fucking time," he growled before kissing her with all the pent-up lust and longing she'd been feeling.

Melting against him, she relished the heat of his big body warming her against the chilly afternoon, her shivers going up in flames with the feel of his rigid cock. "Ben!" she gasped, wrenching her mouth from his when he shoved her jeans down along with her panties, goose bumps breaking out across her exposed buttocks.

"Talk later, this" – he thrust two fingers inside her – "now. You're wet. You want me as much as I want you, have missed me as much, I'll wager."

"Yes, *yes*," she burst out when he spun her around, placed her hands on the rail, and kicked her feet apart. Then he was surging inside her, welcoming her return in the best of ways, leaving no doubt about how much he wanted her.

"Damn it, I love you, Amie," Ben ground out, unable to keep from pounding inside her grasping pussy. *Home, she's finally home.* "Don't you ever leave again, not without me."

"No, I won't," she promised, panting, arching her hips to take his pummeling strokes. "I love you, too."

"Good enough." He gripped her hips, savoring her hot, slick muscles clamping around his hammering girth, milking his seed from his balls until he exploded in a torrent of fiery lust, their groans of pleasure carried away with the slight breeze.

By the time the euphoric fog cleared from his head, the dogs' patience waiting for more of Amie's attention had worn thin. Dancing around them as he adjusted her clothes, tails wagging and yipping with excitement, they were as happy with her return as Ben. He understood close relationships and commitment, which was why he'd let her go without trying harder to talk her into giving them a try. That was a decision she had needed to come to on her own, without pressure from him.

Cupping her face, he kissed her softly, holding her close to whisper against her lips, "Tell me you've returned for more than another vacation."

"Yes, Sir. I've come for as long as you'll have me."

"That works." Slinging an arm around her shoulders, he steered her back to her car, and, from the amount of stuff crammed inside, she had planned for a good long while. It was his job to make sure her sacrifice was worth the risk.

"Go on in. I'll attend to Peaches then get your things."

"Peaches? Your new horse?"

"*Your* new horse. I bought her for you because she can keep up with Thunder."

Shocked pleasure suffused Amie's face, making the mare worth every penny of her price. "You did? You were that sure of my return?"

"Hell no. After talking to Myla, I planned to give you a little more time before coming to get you. I like her, by the way."

A rueful smile curled her soft lips. "So do I.

She never let on. Thank you, for the horse and the second chance."

"You're welcome." He reached up and traced a finger over the dark circle under her left eye, hating seeing evidence of her struggles these past two weeks. But the smile she turned up to him and her pussy's welcoming, wet clasp were proof she was where she wanted to stay.

Six months later

"Father Joe, it's good to see you again." Ben straightened from leaning against the fence and dragged his eyes off Amie to shake the priest's hand. The priest had played an instrumental role in Dakota's relocation to Idaho from Arizona. The rare expression of pleasure reflected on Dakota's dark face when Father Joe had surprised him today had been priceless. "Careful, or your guys may expect you to make the trip more often now that you've proved twice in a month is no hardship."

"I wouldn't mind seeing more of them, especially now that two are married. Besides, I wouldn't have missed seeing Dakota's face when you all surprised him with this reception after he'd whisked Poppy off to Vegas for a quickie wedding to avoid socializing at a big wedding. Shawn should have known his and

Lisa's shindig the first of the month would scare him off." Joe's fond gaze rested on the three men standing at the grill on Shawn's patio.

Taking in the crowd of well-wishers, Ben said, "I half expected him to walk away once he arrived. He probably would have if Poppy weren't so ecstatic to welcome her parents and sister back." The new Mrs. Smith sat at one of the tables with her family and several women, including Amie. "She hasn't stopped smiling all afternoon."

"It's a good day all around, one I wouldn't have missed for the world. Now, If I can talk you into marrying your girl around the time of Clayton's wedding in June, you can save me a trip."

Ben laughed. "If that was supposed to be a subtle hint, you bombed."

Father Joe gave him an unrepentant grin. "No sense beating around the bush."

"Well, stick around. You might get your wish. In the meantime, let's grab one of those buffalo burgers." The surprise on the priest's face was almost as comical as Dakota's earlier.

Spring wildflowers spread a colorful blanket across the surrounding rangeland, and, with the warm afternoon sun shining bright, the late April day had turned out perfect for this gathering of family and friends. Ben thought it was also the perfect time to join the ranks of his fallen Doms and seal his and Amie's relationship. In the last six months, her constant presence had helped fill the void from Bart's passing, her smile enough to lift his spirits, her sexual submission and otherwise independent nature the perfect mix for him.

She had met his parents and sister when they'd come for Thanksgiving, and he'd gone to Omaha with her to spend Christmas with her family. Myla and Matt returned with them, and they'd thrown a New Year's party, everyone welcoming Myla with such enthusiasm, she'd mentioned moving out here. Ben didn't think that would happen anytime soon as there were jobs and families to consider for both of them, whereas Amie could work from anywhere and didn't have to take into account anyone else's work or family when she'd relocated.

"I'll catch you later, Father," he said as they reached the middle of the yard. "I'm going to see what Amie wants to eat."

"You go on, and good luck."

Ben nodded but didn't believe he needed it. He could still read Amie's every expression and knew she was happy here with him and his rescues and their mutual friends, and small-town living that agreed with her. His heartbeat quickened along with his cock as he strode up behind her and took her arm.

"If you'll excuse us," he told the group at the table, "I need to borrow Amie for a few minutes."

"He can borrow me anytime if he looks at me like that." Kathie's voice filtered back to him as he led Amie toward a path bisecting a woody area several yards away from the party.

Chuckling, Amie peered up at him. "Better make sure you don't send one of those hot stares her way."

"No need to worry," he assured her, entering the woods.

Amie's pulse kicked up a notch like it always did whenever Ben approached then touched her. With each passing day, she'd fallen deeper under his spell, discovering more about him to love, succumbing to his sexual creativity with heated arousal only he could sate. The pleasure she'd reaped from living with him had tempered the ache of missing home those first few weeks. But she and Myla still spoke as much as always, and hearing her friend talk about Matt with such love confirmed she'd made the right decision.

“Ben, we can’t just disappear from Poppy and Dakota’s reception,” she complained with a huff as he dragged her far enough into the trees she could no longer see anything else.

“This will only take a minute.”

Stopping at a large, towering pine, he pressed her against the rough bark, her thin blouse offering no comfort. Like always, that didn’t matter as he lowered his head and kissed her with slow, toe-curling thoroughness. But it was his next, gruff, demanding words that triggered her heart into a rapid, blood-pumping rhythm of joy.

“Marry me, Amie.”

“Okay,” she breathed against his mouth without hesitation. After all, he was her perfect Dom cowboy, so what was left to think about?

The End

ABOUT BJ WANE

I live in the Midwest with my husband and our Goldendoodle. I love dogs, enjoy spending time with my daughter, grandchildren, reading and working puzzles.

We have traveled extensively throughout the states, Canada and just once overseas, but I now much prefer being homebody.

I worked for a while writing articles for a local magazine but soon found my interest in writing for myself peaking.

My first book was strictly spanking erotica, but I slowly evolved to writing steamy romance with a touch of suspense. My favorite genre to read is suspense.

I love hearing from readers. Feel free to contact me at bjwane@cox.net with questions or comments.

MORE BOOKS BY BJ WANE

VIRGINIA BLUEBLOODS SERIES

Blindsided
Bind Me to You
Surrender to Me
Blackmailed
Bound by Two

MURDER ON MAGNOLIA ISLAND

Logan
Hunter
Ryder

MIAMI MASTERS SERIES

Bound and Saved
Master Me, Please
Mastering Her Fear
Bound to Submit
His to Master and Own
Theirs To Master

COWBOY DOMS SERIES

Submitting to the Rancher
Submitting to the Sheriff
Submitting to the Cowboy
Submitting to the Lawyer
Submitting to Two Doms
Submitting to the Cattleman
Submitting to the Doctor

COWBOY WOLF SERIES

Gavin
Cody
Drake

DOMS OF MOUNTAIN BEND

Protector
Avenger
Defender

SINGLE TITLES

Claiming Mia
Masters of the Castle: Witness Protection Program
Dangerous Interference
Returning to Her Master
Her Master at Last

CONTACT BJ WANE

Website
bjwaneauthor.com

Twitter
twitter.com/bj_wane

Facebook
www.facebook.com/bj.wane
www.facebook.com/BJWaneAuthor

Bookbub
www.bookbub.com/profile/bj-wane

Instagram
www.instagram.com/bjwaneauthor

Goodreads
www.bit.ly/2S6Yg9F

BJ Wane

Made in United States
North Haven, CT
29 December 2021